Hatred in the blood, love in the heart is a collaborative writing project. The contributors are;

- Dilpreet Bains

- Taranvir Chohan

- Avneet Dhesi

- Harnoor Ghuman

- Jasmeet Khatri

- Amanjot Panesar

- Jessica Sachdeva

- Tegh Sandhu

- Balmeet Sarna

- Manavee Sehdev

- Harpreet Tatla

- Risan Thirupparan

with cover design by Kirandeep Singh and Harnoor Ghuman. The project was overseen by Joe Reddington.

The group cheerfully acknowledges the wonderful help given by Ellie Crompton.

And a big thank you goes to SHINE who funded this wonderful project.

It's been a wonderful opportunity, and everyone involved has been filled with incredible knowledge and enthusiasm.

Finally, we would like to thank all staff at Guru Nanak Sikh Academy for their support in releasing our novelists from lessons for a full week.

The group started to plan out their novel at 9am on Monday 4th July 2016 and completed their last proof reading at 2.30pm on Friday 8th July 2016.

We are incredibly proud to state that every word of the story, every idea, every chapter and yes, every mistake, is entirely their own work. No teachers, parents or other students touched a single key during this process, and we would ask readers to keep this in mind.

We are sure you will agree that this is an incredible achievement. It has been a true delight and privilege to see this group of young people turn into professional novelists in front of our very eyes.

Hatred in the blood, love in the heart

Tim Cooks

Contents

1   Dejected Parents   7

2   51st Mission   15

3   The Malicious Mission   25

4   Friends Before Foes   33

5   An Illusion Of An Illness 39

6   An Adoption Addition   45

7   Perplexing Powers   55

8   Worried For An Unwanted Wish 63

9   A Haunting History   71

10 A Random Reunion   81

11 A Distant Relationship   91

12 Revenge   99

13 Jealousy Kills   105

14 Deceitful Thinking   113

15 Deadly Influences   117

16 Suspections And Suicide   125

17 An Unknown Agent   131

18 Abuse   137

19 Hello Police, Bye Dad   143

20 Mysterious Hackers   151

21 Insert title here   161

22 Masterminds   169

23 The Fatal Injury   179

24 The Evil Is Victorious   189

25 Mistakes And Regret   195

26 Daughter Love   201

27 The Mad Plan   209

28 Crime Cases   215

29 Self Harm   221

30 The Doc Dies   227

31 Back-Stabbing Brother   233

32 The Truth Is Out   241

33 World War III   247

34 Safehouse   255

35 A Sister's Quest   265

36 The Last Phone Call   277

37 Bipolar Disorder wins   283

38 Everything's Gone   287

39 The Remembrance   295

40 Wrong Is Never Right   309

Chapter 1

Dejected Parents

Location:Royal Edinburgh Hospital

Time: 24th June 2016

Tom was relaxing in his hospital room, there was a long day ahead of him. Tom was an unusual boy. He was very secretive and had a very troublesome life. He was 21 years old but he still hadn't developed that maturity yet. He had anger issues and had anxiety and did a lot of self-harm to himself. He was being treated in the Royal Edinburgh Hospital by Ellie, his doctor. Royal Edinburgh Hospital was massive, a very complicated place with many wards and many people that were ill.

Tom was pondering over the reason why he chose to come to this awful place in the middle of the day. He wouldn't have chosen to come over here if life was different for him... if he was one of the popular guys. Most of the people here were like him... and had some sort of mental health illness. People here were screaming in agony and pain, struggling and suffocating. It was hard to get everything in the hospital processed in your mind, so many awful things happened to people and it was very upsetting, it was like they were trapped and had nowhere to go... like him. He thought over what had happened in the morning at his house...

Faint voices in the distance woke Tom up, then those voices turned into screams, and then ear-splitting sounds. Tom wondered who was making all that racket and cautiously tip-toed downstairs. As he got closer to the banister, he realised who was shouting; his parents. Tom got very frustrated and went downstairs, when would his parents learn that their fighting only caused their children to be depressed. Tom's parents were very violent and always abused each other. They would always fight and never give their children the things and attention they needed. They despised each other and didn't want to live together, but they were afraid to be sent to jail, so they never called the police.

He slowly trudged downstairs, just in time to see his dad shout " LEAVE".

Tom wondered what they were fighting about this time, usually his parents fought over useless things such as who would win the football match, where the Olympics should be held and little things like that. There were a few times though, when they had fought over things that actually had a proper reason; when they fought over money. He then heard his mum say "they will definitely remain... if they don't, then I will walk up to the council and shout at them!"

"Yeah, in your dreams, you foul creature!"

"Uh... I'm the same creature as you..."

Tom was just sick of all these useless and pathetic fights...fighting over the EU? Seriously...

Tom couldn't handle it any more. He had enough. He got up from the stairs (he had sat on the stairs because he was THAT tired) and charged into the living room. He started shouting "just be quiet...every day all you guys do is FIGHT, FIGHT, FIGHT and FIGHT!"

That would hopefully stop them fighting for a little while, until they started fighting about who had caused Tom to shout that loud. Tom sighed and slammed the door as hard as he could, with all this force. Tom was just too vexed and irritated. He already had too many troubles in his life; life just couldn't get any worse!

To forget about all these depressing events, he took his bag, packed all his stuff, had a look at the time, (it was already quarter past twelve) and decided it was time to go. He didn't know where to go, if only he had his own house, but he couldn't, not with the problem he had. He needed care and support or he could do foolish things. After several minutes of deciding where to go and coming to no conclusion, he decided to go to the Royal Edinburgh hospital. And that was where he was now.

Tom snapped back to reality as a bird started tweeting loudly. He shook off all the memories and thought of the things that had to be done. After five minutes of relaxing, he inhaled deeply and crawled out of his bed. Tom held the cold door-

knob and stepped outside. He thought of
what to do next and then he dragged himself downstairs as there was nothing better
to do.

As he was descending down the birch
stairs, he saw Audrey waiting for him. Audrey was a boy aged 21 who had Bipolar
disorder. Sometimes he would feel very
happy but then at other times he would
feel very depressed and upset. Audrey hated
getting attention and would sometimes get
depressed when lots of people were near
him as he would want to get out of there.
Audrey was often misunderstood, but with
him and his other two friends, one of which
was Tom, everything was fine. Or was
it? As Tom reached the last stair, he saw
a board of monopoly in Audrey's hands.
Tom knew Audrey wanted to play with

him so they both sat down for a game of
monopoly.

Chapter 2

51st Mission

Location:The Baked Potato Shop

Time: 26th June 2016

When you look at this hideout from outside you will think of it as a normal baked potato shop, but right underneath it is a hideout, not a big hideout because this wasn't the main headquarters of the MI5 but it was still as amazing as the main headquarters because it had all the things an agent could need, guns, bullet-proof vests and many other tools and disguises. Many agents were on computers or got ready for missions and wore disguises and got the necessary tools.

But not this agent, this was George. He was one of the top agents in the MI5 with completed over 50 missions without fail, unlike Hudson who attempted 10 missions and failed every single one and came into the agency with a black eye and a massive concussion. George was walking around the agency seeing if everything was alright. He was walking towards the coffee machine when a deep voice came behind him

"George!" It was the Chief, Chief Rizwan

He was looking quite downhearted; with a sloppy hand gesture he called George to come into his cabin. Then George followed him in.

"Come on in George." with a depressed voice asked Chief Rizwan.

George slowly walked in and asked the Chief

"Are you alright, Sir? I haven't seen you this upset since you lost your wedding ring and drowned your tears with 40 chicken wings.." George said that, with a hope of distracting the chief from his misery but it didn't work. George sat down when the Chief started to talk.

"George, how are you doing?"

"Sir, I'm fit and fine."

"So George, I need to tell you that, I

17

am going to I am going to go for a while."

"Why, sir? Is everything alright?"

"Yeah, it's just that my mother died and there's this very important mission I have to complete, but I was wondering if you could take over it."

"Sure Sir! I would be glad to."

The Chief started to smile. "But, first of all you need to know what the mission is." George was more enthusiastic than ever, ready for anything.

"There is a hitman on the loose, his name is Blood Spirit and he is a known to kill and eat. If he gets paid to kill he will not stop. He has currently destroyed nearly every single orphanage except two and I want you to find out what he is after and for you to stop him ." The Chief handed George a file and told him that

that file was all about Blood Spirit and his past.

Out of nowhere, a siren went off. George started to panic. Then Jeffrey (Agent 010) opened the Chief's door and said,

"He's at it again!" With a small grin, the Chief looked at George.

"You're up!" George got up and out of his seat and went to Jeffrey, he asked him who was Blood Spirit and up to, Jeffrey told him that Blood Spirit attacked another orphanage.

"Another one!?!?" replied George.

"And we have no clue why."

The Chief came up behind George and explained to him that that was the reason we need an agent like him to stop a criminal like Blood Spirit.

Confused and baffled, George was going mental just trying to think about the reason behind Blood Spirit destroying all the orphanages in Edinburgh.He rushes to the chief and talks to him.

"Chief, I can't do this."

"You're giving up so early."

"Chief, I just don't why he's doing this. WHY!"

"Instead of looking at why, why don't you look at what does he get from it. He is not eating anyone so he is probably trying to find something."

"Sir, you're right!"

"What do you mean?"

"Sorry Sir, bye!"

George was shocked that even a criminal like Blood Spirit would have such a small heart that he would hurt children that are misfortunate. He couldn't get his mind to think of why he was doing this, but then he had an idea, he called the orphanage that had been attacked and asked them if they have seen something or heard something why Blood Spirit was doing this. He tried several orphanages before one was just stuck on saying a word Kylie. He was confused why the care lady was saying that and he cut the call.

George calls the last orphanage and told them that they needed to be safe. He told them that there was a murderer on the loose and he was looking for something. He starts to ask them about any one related to Harry Scott(Blood Spirit) because Harry used to be an orphan at the age of 16 and he has changed since his mother was killed. George was giving them advice how to keep the house secure and he told them not to let any stranger come in.

He was about to cut the call but he remembered that the previous care worker was saying Kylie and George quickly asked her about Kylie and she said that,

"She is an orphan living here." George was shocked to hear this because this opened a new angle to this case.

He kept on talking about Kylie and was asking the care worker about who was she. He was told that,

"She is a 18 years old girl who is mentally disabled, and because of that her parents left her in front of a police station when she was very young and the police found her."

"They kept her for 1 week and contacted the social workers. Then she had been here since then. She had been through a really tough life. Her parents didn't want her and they said she was a pain." George thanks her for the information and cuts the call.

He thought about Kylie and then he understood that Blood Spirit wasn't looking for something but someone; Kylie.He rushed towards the chief's office but he wasn't there.He got his phone and called the Chief telling him that:

"Blood Spirit isn't after something, but he is trying to find Kylie, a girl in the Dean Orphanage, but I am not sure why!"

The chief replied "Wha What you talking about and if that's the case you would have to save her. Get her before an innocent girl's life is lost and Blood Spirit escapes."

"Yes sir, I am going to her now" said

George.

Chapter 3

The Malicious Mission

Location:Under Edinburgh Castle

Time: 28th June 2016

Under Edinburgh castle was Blood spirit's

hideout, a very spooky place which was very old and hadn't been cleaned for years. It looked quite ancient as there were many broken things, half of them fallen apart and withered in time. Also there were antiques that costed a fortune, very special and rare. All over the hideout you could see many computers everywhere with plans, plans of destruction. The hideout was massive, you couldn't see the end of it. Blueprints stuck on the walls, viewing the plan on how to destroy Edinburgh and Kylie.

"Welcome Ellie!" growled Blood spirit "I was waiting for you!"

Ellie jumped as she heard his voice reflecting off of all of the walls in the room. She looked all over but she couldn't find him.

"Behind you young lady!" The same

voice boomed

She instantly turned around now, her eyes as big as saucers.

He quickly tied her onto a chair and grinned.

"So Ellie, I need you to be in my master plan." he wickedly gave her a evil smile.

Blood Spirit was circling her, spinning his hand with the knife that usually had its place in Blood Spirits top pocket. "So, Ellie I could use your services now. This plan might be the best plan Blood Spirit has ever thought of and I need your help to pull the plan into place." He said

"Ellie, you must do this job right" he said slyly. "Or else!" he said clinging onto the knife making his own hand bleed with sticky, red human blood. Ellie had no words. She was frightened so she just nodded and agreed to do whatever he said.

"And" he growled. "If you dare tell anyone" he came close to her pale face and whispered in her ear, "you know what will happen, don't you?" his breath was warm and Ellie noticed a small scar underneath his eye. Ellie was numb with fear as this happened.

"If you don't get this job done or betray me I'm afraid I will have to let you go on a permanent holiday, to heaven, or hell if you prefer." Blood Spirit said while a shiver ran down Ellie's spine. He then, out of nowhere, hurled the knife at the wall behind Ellie and it hit the wall with a thud. Ellie was petrified so petrified that she would

"This plan is resting in yours and Tom's shoulders now, I am handing over total control over this plan to you both. You better not tell anyone, I really need this" Blood Spirit said. Ellie's spine. Blood Spirit never said he had fears, however, even though he will never say it, Blood Spirit was scared of the fact that Ellie might tell someone of his plan and then he might land back in jail.He ran the blade of the knife down Ellie's back and said in a hushed voice "I trust you, Ellie"

"Maybe I should tell Kylie" Thought Ellie, anxious about what she should do in this blood-curdling situation. She thought about it and wondered. In the end she was agitated about depriving her life so she just agreed to Blood spirit's plan

"Okay, I won't tell anyone" she said gloomily, her face as dark as coal, tears dripping from her face.

"Good" he grizzled. "You better not, or we won't see you tomorrow, and your family the day after!"

She gulped, extremely petrified, her body rigid with fear.

"He doesn't know I want to tell Kylie" she murmured to herself, wiped her tears, her eyes red and sore. She could still feel the place where Blood spirit ran the knife down her back, it was sharp and cold. "I should tell, but what if he finds out. I can't put myself and my family at risk. But someone will die either way, what on earth should I do!!" she was puzzled and wondered why she had to be a part of this mysterious game of hatred and jealousy...

"If you do this job there might be a few thousands in it for you. Don't give me that murky face." he boomed and left.I'd

rather die than get paid for doing crime Ellie thought to herself confused and unsure
what to do.

Chapter 4

Friends Before Foes

Location:Royal Edinburgh Hospital

Time: 30th June 2016

Kylie just entered the hospital room when

Tom got a chance card, Go to Jail'. Tom got really angry but he still continued playing. Audrey rolled a five and purchased Bond Street.' Tom paid fifty and got released from Jail. Audrey then rolled a one which made him land on the hotel that Tom had bought so he had to pay a big amount of money which made Audrey really frustrated that he called the game off. After all this, Audrey then greeted Kylie properly after five minutes of her standing and doing nothing but watching them playing. Kylie was also a patient in the Royal Edinburgh hospital. She had Alice in Wonderland syndrome which caused her to see things in different sizes. Kylie was around the same age as Tom who was 21, but Kylie was three years younger; she was 18.

"Hi." Audrey said to Kylie.

"Hi Audrey, how are you?"

"I'm good, it's just Tom...you know how he can be like."

"Yeah, he can be a bit rude sometimes."

"Hmmm..."

The conversation ended when Tom started shouting

"Audrey! Why can't you ever play a game properly...just because you lost!"

Audrey got very irritated by this so she shouted,

"Alright then Tom! Why don't you play with Kylie then...we'll see who wins this round!"

Tom accepted this challenge and smirked as he knew that he would obviously win this game as easily as he had won the game with Audrey.

Kylie sat down on the floor and chose the dog as her player and started by rolling a five. The game started off with Tom clearly winning but then tables started to turn; Tom got sent to jail three times in a row!

"Now who's losing?"

Audrey exclaimed as loud as he could.

"SHUT UP!"

Tom screamed as a social worker hurriedly rushed past, hushing all three. They ended the game after two rounds and started to count their money. To make sure they didn't cheat, Audrey counted the money. When he finished counting, Tom had $551 while Ky$ Kylie won the overall game which made Tom so angry that he threw the porcelain vase on the floor and ran upstairs to his room.

"He's just like that...but it's nothing he can change, don't worry about it."

Audrey whispered as he saw Kylie biting her nails anxiously.

"I hope I haven't upset him too much, I should never have played! I felt dizzy anyways and kept thinking the dice was half the size of what it actually was!"

Audrey tried his best to console Kylie and then she then came to a conclusion that maybe it actually wasn't her fault. Kylie then changed the topic and started talking to Audrey about their social workers. None of them mentioned Tom after that.

When they had nothing to talk about, there was an awkward silence between them. After several minutes of sitting and doing nothing in particular, a doctor called

Kylie into his room to talk about her illness. Kylie waved to Audrey and went into the room. Audrey was starting to feel depressed and upset for no specific reason, but to try to feel a bit better, he went upstairs to his room and started colouring in his colouring book. However it wasn't working and he was starting to become angry so he tried to calm down and decided to sleep. Tomorrow would be another day.

Chapter 5

An Illusion Of
An Illness

Location:Royal Edinburgh Hospital

Time: 3rd July 2014

The dark horrible room consisted entirely of a table, three chairs and three people. One man, one woman and one boy around 19 years old.

"Who's going to be the fake friend?" Said a young boy who had a high voice.

"We could always use our leader; he is the youngest." Replied a voice, female this time.

"Ellie, you will have to become a doctor for a day, and get him into hospital" said the deep voice and it pointed at the petrified woman in the corner.

"Certainly" Ellie said.

"So when you get there I want you to say to the staff that he has anxiety" Said the deep, fearful voice once again.

"Is this really necessary sir? "Said Ellie.

"Of course, how else would I become

the most powerful man in the world?" shouted the deep voice.

"Of course sir." Replied the woman.

Thoughts were racing through Ellie's mind. What would happen to her if she didn't get the job done? What if the hospital people didn't believe her?

Later on in the day, Ellie was dressed in a white coat- like a doctor. She was ready to take Tom to the hospital.

She arrived at the desk where there was a tall receptionist standing.

"Tom must be taken into the hospital immediately." Ellie demanded.

"And where is your doctor ID?" Asked the receptionist.

"Here." Ellie said and she pulled out a fake ID.

"What illness does he have?" Asked the

receptionist.

"Anxiety." Replied Ellie with any hesitation.

"What were the dates of observations?" asked the receptionist.

"24th- 26th of June" She said as if she had rehearsed it before.

"Just through there." The receptionist pointed towards the ward on the right.

They walked into the ward and there were children playing and talking. Two of them looked around the boy's age (Audrey and Kylie). At the end of the ward there were two chairs where they sat down.

"Here is a picture of her. Make sure you don't mess this up, you're the one who has their job on the line." Said Ellie.

"It's fine, Boss trusts me." Tom replied

After Ellie gave the picture of Kylie to

Tom she went through the plan. "So all that you have to do is make friends with and get as close as possible because we need lots of information. Once that is done your job is complete, I will then take over and act as her doctor and take a sample of her DNA and then take it back to boss."

"OK, OK I've got it; after all I was one of the main mastermind of the plan."

"OK then, bye" Ellie said whilst getting up from the chair.

The boy looked at the picture and then looked up to see the same person talking with her friend on the other side of the room. Remembering the plan, he got up and walked over there. "Hi, my name is Tom."

"Hi my name is Kylie and this is my friend Audrey." Said the girl from the picture.

"Hi" Said Audrey in a very timid voice.

"What are you in for?" Asked Kylie.

"Anxiety "Tom replied, quickly on the spot.

"I'm here for Bipolar disorder" Said Audrey.

"And I'm here for, Alice in wonderland syndrome."Said Kylie

Chapter 6

An Adoption Addition

Location: baked potato shop

Time: 4th July 2016

George was on his phone, and he found

out the address of the Dean orphanage: 76 Willowbrae Rd, Edinburgh EH8 7HA, where Kylie lived most of her life. George went on google maps and saw that it was 50 miles away! So he chose a car which had a higher speed than all others, none other than the Auto Ricksha! He got in and checked if he got everything he needed and noticed that he had left his gun! He quickly rushed back and took a pistol and an assault rifle, quickly got into the car and rushed off with his Auto Rickshaw.

He zoomed through the streets of Edinburgh way over the speed limit. George was worried and was thinking very negatively, he thought to himself miserably, "What if she had been taken already by Blood Spirit? If I get that Blood Spirit would kill him brutally until every drop of his blood is taken out of his body."

The way he thinks just shocks me the most, how could any human think like that? Suddenly he noticed that the police tried to stop him because he was going way over the speed limit! He stopped and they came towards him.

"You were going way over the speed limit so I will give you a fine!"

George just had to hold up his identity card and the police apologised and left.

He kept going in his Auto Rickshaw and he just couldn't get Blood Spirit out of his mind. He was so angry that he didn't know what punishment he would give him when he got him because that's how evil he was. He keeps going and he gets a call from the chief Rizwan and he said, "Why did you go by car? There is a helicopter

coming to you just go to the nearest port
that you know, it will be much quicker."

"Thanks, boss."

"It's alright, take care, bye!" and he
sped off to the nearest port.

He was on his way to the nearest port,
which actually wasn't that close because
it was 20 miles away! But because the
car he chose, the Auto Rickshaw he could
make it to the port much quicker than
any normal car could. On the way, the
thought about what type of child Kylie
would be and time flied past so quickly
that he reached the port even quicker than
he thought he would. He got off his Auto
Rickshaw, remembered to take his guns
and ran towards the port and saw the helicopter waiting for him to come so George
quickly got in and they set off to the or-

phanage.

The helicopter was even faster than the Auto Rickshaw. He started wondering how long he would stay in MI5, he had been an agent for a long time and he thought about living a normal life for the rest of his life. But he knew that the MI5 needed him or he would have left quite a while ago. He could see the orphanage from quite a far distance away.

"How long is it going to take to get there?" asked George.

The driver said "Around 2 minutes."

A few minutes later, we were there and the driver dropped down a ladder and I got down. He had to walk for 5 minutes because he was dropped off a little further away from the orphanage.

Once he was there it was dusk and the

sun was going down. He went into the orphanage to the manager's office to speak to him.

"Hi, my name is George and I am from the MI5 it's nice to meet you."

He shakes his hand. "I am here to take a child from this orphanage, her name is Kylie."

George Exclaimed. "Why?" said Christopher (the manager).

"Because there is an evil person trying to take her but we don't know why." George explained.

"Ok, please take her to safety. From here take a right and go straight and her room is room 5." Said Christopher "Thanks." said George.

He started walking towards Kylie's room to meet her. He goes in the room and wakes her up and she is in shock.

"Who are you?" said Kylie.

"Hi, my name is George and I am now your father." George said.

"What?" said Kylie nervously.

"Come on, let's go." George said.

"Ok, wait but where are we going?"

"You are going to live with me from now on so you're coming to my house. I am in a hurry so quickly change your clothes so we can go!" Kylie changed her clothes and they hurried out.

As they rushed outside George took out his phone and called for a taxi because if he went in a helicopter Kylie would get suspicious. He wanted Kylie to see him as a normal man who runs a baked potato shop so she doesn't get involved with the agent things he does. He wanted his daughter to live a normal life. The taxi had come and we both got in. George introduced himself properly to Kylie.

"Hey, I am George and I'm 49 years old and I run a baked potato shop." George said.

Once they got home Kylie wanted to look around the baked potato shop. She just couldn't believe someone would actually come to the orphanage to get her especially, she never expected anyone to come and get her. Now that she had a father she could live a normal life, go to school and have friends. George then took her and showed her her room and it was really big. She wanted to thank him but he said that he had to go somewhere and he left. George had actually went to the MI5 hideout to hack into the orphanage systems to get all the information about Kylie.

George got all the information that he needed about Kylie. He was just about to leave the hideout when he got a phone call from Christopher.

"Hi it's George speaking."

"Oh thank goodness my orphanage has been attacked; someone called Blood Spirit said that he wanted Kylie and I told him that I didn't know where she was so then he beat me up and made my orphanage a big mess! You have to help me please, stop him for me and get him in prison!"

"Ok, ok just calm down a bit and don't worry I am already on his trail and I'll do better than getting him into prison; I will kill him."

Chapter 7

Perplexing Powers

Location:School, George's House

Time: 6th July 2016

Kylie was walking to school. Suddenly

a group of bullies appeared in front of her. Kylie knew these people, they had been teasing her since primary school. They were the strongest but not the cleverest kids in her class. Kylie was the smartest person in the class and the bullies were jealous. They were girls, who thought that they were popular and pretty and clever, in reality it was the opposite.

"You can't be popular. You're a weirdo and a nerd!" shouted Sam.

"Yeah." sang one of the girls from the back.

"No, I'm not." replied Kylie "At least I am not as dumb as you whos in set 7 for everything."

Sam's face turned red; she was clearly quite angry and embarrassed.

"I am not the one with the mental illness, if you forgot!" screamed Sam.

"So, at least I wasn't rejected 2 times by two boys" said Kylie

"Who rejected me? Liar." replied Sam, her cheeks were turning red at this point.

"Josh and Harry!" Screamed Kylie

Sam had enough of this and she pushed Kylie to the floor; she started crying.

Then all of sudden, Sam started to levitate off the floor. Sam started to scream. The other's tried to pull her down but she was too high up. Sam was quite big but the others were quite short and wimpy. Sam flew straight into a dumpster and started crying. The others ran to help her up. Sam was dizzy and they all realised that it was Kylie who had down this. The other's waited for Sam to go and beat her up but Sam had a different idea. To Run!

All four of them started to run but they all started to levitate. They tried to fly to the ground but they were too high in the sky. Kylie had her eyes closed and tears were pouring down her cheeks. All she wanted was to be somewhere, to not be Kylie and most of all to not have a mental illness. One by one the bullies started to fly into the dumpster. Lastly Samantha was thrown very hard into the dumpster. Very loud moans from the dumpster forced Kylie to open her eyes. She was amazed to see that the bullies were nowhere to be found. At first she thought that someone had helped her but there was no-one. Her instinct forced her to do one thing, to run.

Kylie stopped running when she thought that she was a good distance away. She thought to herself "What happened there?"

This was the only thing on her mind. As she was thinking, in the corner of her eye, she could see a black bin bag; it had a massive rip in its side probably due to a cat. The bin bag was glowing a turquoise colour, which coincidently was Kylie's favourite colour. She went closer to investigate and was shocked at what happened next, it was floating!

She was so surprised that she nearly fell backwards. She thought that this might be the reason that the bullies went there. She turned back and sprinted to George's house. When she was little her parents left her near a police station. She went to an orphanage, she hated it there everyone teased her. Until George adopted her and that's when her life changed for the better. George was nice and caring. If Kylie asked for anything, George would get it for her.

Back home, Kylie raced to her room. It was quite late and George was making dinner. He was a really good cook and he made delicious Blueberry pie. His secret was that he put a bit of raspberry and strawberry in it. Kylie's room was big, it was 10 times better than her room in the orphanage. The orphanage was called Dean Orphanage. It was an old castle, which was converted into an orphange.It was way to packed and rooms where shared by two people. Her roommate was called Elektra, who was the bad girl of the orphanage. Elektra would steal things and play pranks on the other's. When George went to adopt Kylie, she didn't see what method of transport he used and when they went home, we went by taxi. Kylie did not know how he could afford to pay for a 50 mile journey when he worked in a potato shop but she didn't care, she was just happy that he had adopted her. In her room she was thinking about what had happened when one of her toys, Amy, started to float. She pulled her down and cuddled her. Kylie was smart enough to know that she was doing this but she did not know how. She started to look at her books on her shelf. She concentrated hard and eventually was able to make it float. With a flick of her head, she sent it flying. She did this with her coat, her toys, her books and her posters.

"Dinner's ready!" shouted George and Kylie ran downstairs. She could smell the blueberry pie from upstairs.

Chapter 8

Worried For An Unwanted Wish

Location:Baked potato Shop

Time: 6th July 2016

"Woah just imagine levitating objects

with your mind?" Kylie had thought to herself.

"I could change the world, I could have lots of friends after telling everyone, life would be so much easier for me as I could move the T.V remote whenever I'm not bothered to get up. What will my friends think when I tell them this? Would they report it straight away? I don't know what to do!" Kylie exclaimed.

She forces herself to only use the powers for good and fighting evil. Kylie felt like she was kind of like superhero. Kylie went to her room and lies down on her pretty pink bed and thinks.

"Thank you Kylie for saving the day! You're my idol Kylie!" imagining all the fame got Kylie excited and was ready for the future. But to all the fame there were some negatives as there would be some haters so finally she convinced herself that she will keep her own secret.

She wouldn't even tell George as he may not want her anymore because George will give the new start to her life which she needed. She thought that if she had told George he would think that she is very creepy and should be left to rot in the crummy care home. Her future was in sight and she couldn't have just let it go away. Being an orphan is quite sad as u don't have a career who usually takes cares of your needs which every child should have. What would you do, if you have a condition which you have but you don't tell your foster parent who may not adopt you if you tell them? Would you tell them?

Later on, Kylie decided to mess around

with her new powers in her room and got a hand of levitating objects. The levitation had the best of her which may have caused her to make a mess of her room as she had made a mess of the clothes on the floor; the TV was dangling on the wall in a bent way. The state of her room was abhorrent, so abhorrent that even a hobo would not sleep in that room.

After playing around for a few hours she had called it a night. Tomorrow would be a new day and was worried if she could tell Tom and Audrey. If she did, she could have been used as a lab rat or as a possession which would make her very miserable. But best friends tell each other everything even the biggest secrets we don't tell our own parents, so she was in a situation where she didn't know what to do.

She could either go by her instincts and not tell them or just trust Tom and Audrey. The next day was going to be a rollercoaster, things could either go really well with Tom and Audrey or the world falls on her feet.

It's a new day and Kylie decides to tell Tom and Audrey that she has an incredible power which was very shocking at first for Tom and Audrey.

"Hahahaha, are you ok Kylie?What has got into you?" laughed Tom. Kylie tried very hard to prove that she had powers but she had no luck at that moment.

" You're trying to say that you can levitate objects?" questioned Audrey.

"Yes exactly!" said Kylie. The fact that Kylie was getting serious made her friends laugh even more which made Kylie even more angry because no one was believing her. Especially her friends, who were the ones who had to listen and support her.

"I've had enough now, you want proof?" shouted Kylie. Kylie levitated a table and Tom's and Audrey's mouths drop.

"You weren't joking after all then" said Tom. Kylie started to show more levitating tricks and Tom and Audrey applaud.

"We got a friend who can levitate things!" screamed Tom.

"Shush, I don't want anyone to know, " whispered Kylie

Kylie and Audrey had left Tom by himself. So Tom decided to make a phone call. The phone call was to Blood Spirit, the biggest hitman in Edinburgh. Tom was fascinated by Kylie's powers which had made him jealous and wanted it for himself. If Kylie died, he would get the powers. It was set for Tom to carry on being her friend'. So the change in the story began, friends backstabbing each other and wanting them dead.

Chapter 9

A Haunting History

Location:Royal Edinburgh Hospital

Time: 8th July 2016

When Kylie arrived back from Royal

Edinburgh Hospital, she rushed to her bedroom to play.

"Where's George?" she wondered.

When she reached her bedroom she saw
George sitting on her bed waiting for her.
George beckoned to her and told her that
he wanted to have a chat with her.

Kylie felt anxious and was bewildered
as she thought that George would send her
back to the orphanage. This may have
sounded absurd, as George was a really
good person and everyone wanted to get
adopted by him because he was fit and
very kind, so then she reconsidered and
thought that was probably unlikely as she
remembered when he had taken Kylie to
an amusement park and Kylie had told everyone at the orphanage.

"How is the medication going?" asked

George.

"Fine, why?" replied Kylie curiously.

"Oh, nothing I just wanted to know how it was going. Have you made any new friends here?" inquired George.

"Yes, I have. I met them at the hospital. One is called Audrey and the other is called Tom. Tom has a lot of ego and he is quite arrogant when he plays games but usually he's a nice and kind person. Audrey is nice and polite but is mostly sad and she doesn't like to get attention from other people." answered Kylie.

"I know Tom!" said George.

"Oh really, how do you know him?" asked Kylie with a sense of excitement.

"His mom is a regular at the potato shop, occasionally he comes with her." replied George "He seems like a nice kid. His mum certainly thinks so, she's always boasting about how he got good marks or that he got a medal on sports day. However, there are some rumours that Tom's dad abuses his wife."

"If Tom's dad did abuse his wife, Tom would never mention it or talk about it." Replied Kylie, who had now seen Tom in a different way.

"Some kids don't like talking about it." Answered George. "It can be very traumatising, kids cope with it in different ways."

"Why are you behaving so differently since you started going to the hospital?" asked George, who has seen a difference in her behaviour.

Before she would spend a lot of time studying and she would not go out. She would only go out to get something that she really needed. Nowadays, it's the opposite; she never seemed to study and spent hours outside.

"I don't get what you mean, I'm absolutely fine." replied Kylie in an alarmed tone.

What was George talking about? She was still the same Kylie that he had adopted.

"It's just that, when I adopted you were always studying and Christopher told me all about you." said George.

"What did he say about me?" demanded Kylie.

Christopher was the owner of the orphanage. He was a shady and vain person who only cared about money. No-one at the orphanage liked him; all the money the government gave to the orphanage, Christopher would keep most of it. He would buy really cheap food in bulk just so that he could save money and this meant that a lot of the kids were malnourished and skinny.

"That you were the smartest person there and never really went out, but these days you've turned to pretty much the opposite." replied George reluctantly.

"Oh, I guess I have become more independent but I'm okay. I've just been hanging around with my new friends more often." replied Kylie, anxiously hoping that George would accept the lie.

"Do you like it here?" asked George.

"Of course!" replied Kylie "This is way better than the orphanage because I have a full room and it's not split. There aren't bullies teasing me."

"Most people who are bullies are jealous of you and they want to be as smart as you." answered George.

"So everyone that has ever bullied me, was jealous of me?" replied Kylie, who now was happy as this meant that it wasn't her fault that people bullied her.

"You know the orphanage got destroyed!" replied George sadly.

"WHAT!" shouted Kylie. She had had always hated the orphanage. She hated everything about it but she never wanted for it to get destroyed. "What is going to happen to the kids?" asked Kylie.

"They're going to be moved to somewhere else." replied George in a casual voice. "Ok, I'm going down to make dinner; I'll call you down when it's ready"

When George went downstairs to cook dinner, he decided to make spaghetti and meatballs because Kylie said it was her favourite. Meanwhile, upstairs Kylie started thinking about her illness. She had been diagnosed with Alice in Wonderland Syndrome. It's a mental illness associated with migraines. It's when you perceive objects to be smaller, bigger, closer or further than they really are.

It had developed later in her life. Kylie knew exactly why. In the orphanage she could never sleep because either Elektra was talking to one of her friends or someone was crying for their parents.

"Dinner's ready, Sweetie!" shouted George, putting the spaghetti onto the plates and bringing out forks and ketchup.

Kylie rushed down the stairs. The carpet was a bright blood red. In the hall there was a massive TV (A Samsung 52" smart

TV). Kylie loved George but had grown very suspicious of him. He worked in a potato shop and yet a 52 inch TV and such a fancy house. The spaghetti and meatballs was extremely delicious. For dessert they had chocolate ice cream each. Then Kylie went back to her room and drifted off to sleep in the blink of an eye.

Chapter 10

A Random Reunion

```
Location:Audrey's house
```

```
Time: 10th July 2016
```

The doorbell rang. Audrey wasn't expecting any guests that day. However, the 10th July 2016, had turned from an ordinary day into a special day. Audrey cautiously opened the door. At that moment, he was overwhelmed with happiness. His sister, Faith, was on the doormat with a big smile on her face. She ran and hugged Audrey with all her might. He felt as if his body was being constricted by a python.

"Audrey! It feels so good to meet you after ages! How long has it been? Six, seven years?" said Faith.

"I don't know, you tell me." said Audrey. His face lighting up, like a little boy receiving a present at Christmas. He felt over the moon since he had been waiting for his sister for many years.

"MUM!" shouted Faith.

"DAD!" She looked all around the house

but no sign of her parents. "Auds, where's mum and dad?" she looked at him waiting for an answer.

"They left." replied Audrey.

"What do you mean they left?" Faith gazed at him, shocked.

"I mean, they left me."

"Why?"

"They left me after you went to become a lawyer. I was only fifteen. They said they were going on vacation and said they would be back in a couple weeks. Well it seems those few weeks haven't finished."

"How did you survive for so long?"

She didn't know that she was so ignorant and unaware of what was going on in her.

"Well, there are social workers that come every weekend and drop off food. They also pay for the flat bills and the electricity bills." he muttered sadly.

Feeling weak that he couldn't even pay for things that belonged to him.

"I guess you won't need them anymore since I'm here." she said proudly "How come your mood is always changing?" asked Faith worriedly.

"Well, that's just a case of my bipolar disorder." said Audrey. "Mum and dad didn't leave me for nothing. It was because I was diagnosed with bipolar disorder a month after you left."

"Wait, you have bipolar disorder?"

"Yeah, I don't know how I was diagnosed but I just got it and they say the cause is unknown yet."

"I never thought they would do anything like that."

"They're animals. Lazy parents. That's what they are!"

"Well they are still our mum and dad at the end of the day. Think about how much they did for us."

"You mean how much they had done for you. You were always their favourite. You were always treated better. You were always their favourite!" shouted Audrey.

There was an awkward silence between them...no-one knew what to say next.

"Audrey I'm so sorry"

Salty tears dropped from both their eyes.

"Never think like that." said Faith.

"Well it's just the bitter truth." said Audrey.

"Sometimes in life we just have to move on from the bad things and think about the positives in life. They were one of the bad things. Just remember whenever something bad happens to you, something good always comes out of it."

"Well, by the way things have been going in my life that is true because now I have got you to look after me."

Audrey was overwhelmed with happiness. Tears of happiness now grew in his eyes. He had never felt like this since his first memories.

"I have something else to tell you. Far worse than mum and dad leaving." said Audrey.

"What can possibly be worse than parents leaving their son by himself who has bipolar disorder." replied Faith now feeling anxious on what he was going to say.

"The thing is, if it wasn't for those social workers I would be in heaven right now. Honestly, I have attempted suicide multiple times."

"Woah Woah! Are you mad?!"

"Yeah, I think so. I didn't want to live with myself but now since you are here those feelings are fading away. It is in the past. It is behind me like a ponytail."

Faith laughed at the joke even though it wasn't something to laugh at. But that was just Faith. She would never understand her own people.

"Is pizza still your favourite food?" asked Faith.

"Yeah! Obviously! What else is better than pizza?!" exclaimed Audrey.

"I'll take that as yes then."

"Why do you ask?"

"Because I'm going to make some! Duh!"

"That's a relief, I was just going to or-der some. That's saves me some money!"

Audrey was in the clouds. It was the most special day for him. However, that would gradually change. His life was about to turn over. This excitement wasn't going to last forever. He tried to enjoy it for as long as he hoped it would last.

"So how was life without mum and dad?" asked Faith.

"It was boring but fine. I would rather live by myself than with people who don't care about me. I usually spend all my time at the hospital and have therapy for my bipolar disorder." replied Audrey. "How was life training to be a lawyer?"

"It was good. I just finished my course. I'm trying to find a firm. I thought I would come here to stay here until I can afford a place to stay. I thought mum and dad would be here but clearly they're not!" She said sadly.

"It wasn't easy just with the social workers around. I was also bullied when I went to high school. That's why I paid attention to all my studies, so I could quickly get out of school. I just stay home and indoors now. I don't even remember what the sun looks like anymore!" said a sad and depressed Audrey, the one that was unknown.

"What would you do if there was a cure for bipolar disease?" asked Faith.

"I really couldn't do anything because there are 5.7 million people with bipolar disorder and I'm no one special." replied Audrey.

"Well you are special in my eyes. You are special to everyone who cares about you. I would do anything to get that cure for you because you're my brother."

"Thank you. It's nice knowing that someone cares about me. Hmm..., I wonder how you have ever showed me that you care about me. Let me think. Well, you left me when I was a kid??"

Tears grew in Audrey's eyes. He didn't know how to react. If there was a cure he would be so happy and would love his life. He forgave his parents for leaving him sometimes, Audrey could understand their point of view and sometimes he didn't even want to live with himself. But with the cure...maybe his parents might come back?

Chapter 11

A Distant Relationship

```
Location:Audrey's house
```

```
Time: 12th July 2016
```

Faith entered the room and saw Audrey

sitting down feeling depressed.

"What's wrong?" she questioned him.

He just shook his head, and closed his eyes, rubbing his hands together. Faith gazed at her brother. They did look alike a lot, but she just didn't want to admit it. His curly blonde hair, her blonde smooth locks, they could almost have been twins, except the five years age difference. Audrey asked her about how her life was before she came back.

"Well" she started off "before I came back, I was off fulfilling my dream of becoming a lawyer. It was very hard work; however, I feel like I have fully tried my hardest and become the best I possibly could!"

She looked at him, and he looked at her, but the look wasn't a proud one. He didn't have a twinkle his eyes that a little brother has when his older sister achieves something.

"Anyways" Faith sighed. "Audrey, I have a question for you, but I don't want you to feel like this question is really pressurizing" she stared at him.

"Go on..." he muttered.

"Um, it's just.., well, " she looked deep into his blue swirly eyes "Where are mum and dad exactly?" she whispered.

There was a dead silence. Nothing was in movement, everything was as still as a statue, frozen.

"Mum" Audrey said.

The way he said this specific word was different. It was as if he wasn't angry, nor upset and sad. He said this word as if he felt disappointed.

"Mum, " he repeated. "I don't even know" he whispered, a tear rolled down his eye. "They gave no address before they left. They said they were going on a holiday and then just left with their stuff, I told you, remember? No one cares about me or actually wants me, I'm just unwanted Audrey, that no one likes or bothers about!"

Faith stared at him. She had returned back to him. Did that mean nothing to him?

"Audrey! she cried "I've come back, I'm your sister, I'll never leave you."

"But you did" he whispered. "I was only 5 and you left. All you cared about was your dream. I had a dream too, to spend my childhood with my older sister, my inspiration, but now I feel like I don't have a sister and I never did."

Those phrases felt like a bang in the heart for Faith. She wiped her tears and leaned in closely to Audrey.

"You wouldn't have understood Audrey." she pleaded. "But don't say that"

"Wouldn't have understood what? That you left me for your selfishness and you didn't care about your little brother?"

"Audrey" sighed Faith "It was different".

"I didn't want a little baby brother's responsibility on my shoulders!" she stammered "and I know it sounds selfish, but I have a life of my own as well, and I wanted to live it, I don't understand why sometimes you can't live your life and be happy." She didn't know how to say it any more kinder. She knew those words sounds ever so harsh, but she couldn't lie to him. "If I stayed, I would have had to look after you. And as you grew older you would have grown more attached to me, and stopped me from fulfilling my dreams. I didn't want that; I wanted us both to be happy" she whispered and closed her eyes and whimpered.

"Ok" Audrey squeaked as he burst into tears.

Faith tried to cuddle up close to him but he shuffled away and out of the room. He sniffed as he went into the faint kitchen and sobbed on his own. Faith felt so awful, she didn't know what to do.

.

"I'm the worst sister ever!" she moaned.

She was confused, how could she help her brother?

She went into the kitchen where Audrey

quickly wiped his salty tears.

"I'll make lunch for us." she spluttered.

"It's fine, you don't need to. You didn't even bother making that pizza you said earlier. Fake promises don't mean anything. Before you left me you said you will come back quickly, couldn't keep that promise either? Don't make promises you know you won't be able to keep, because it won't affect you, but it hurts other people!"

The last time she made food he was 4. She took the bread and salad and made him a sandwich. Audrey choked and couldn't eat it.

"What's wrong Auds?"

"I- I'm just not used to your food anymore!" he stormed.

"Auds, listen, don't worry, I'll make it

all better, I'm going to make up all the time we lost, I will make everything better. I know you won't believe me, but don't I deserve a bit of trust? You know I love you loads, and I've changed."

"Are you done saying words you're not going to keep?" He whispered.

She didn't know what else to say.

Chapter 12

Revenge

```
Location:Under Edinburgh castle
```

```
Time: 14th July 2016
```

"I miss you mum" Blood Spirit said to himself.

He had never really spent that much

time with his mum and he regretted it. He was alone and had no one to receive love from and to share his feelings with. Now he would have flashbacks of his mum and the few moments he had with her. Blood Spirit never used to care that much about his mum but now he realised how important she was. He wished he could go back and spend more time with her and appreciate her more than he really did. But he knew it couldn't happen.

There was one day that Blood Spirit remembered most of all. It was the day of his mum's funeral. He remembered that day. It was that one day that turned his life upside down and ever since then he had totally changed as a person. It was like something clicked inside him and changed him forever.

"MUM WHERE ARE YOU!?" He screamed to himself.

His eyes poured with tears. He was trembling. There he sat in the dark corner of his hideout under the Castle Of Edinburgh. Now he was just screaming as if he had run out of tears. He just missed her so much.

Another moment was when he was told that his mum was murdered. Blood Spirit's heart sank deeper than it had ever sunk before. At that moment he just changed as a human.

"Why does it hurt so much" he thought to himself. "Would my mum want me to be sat here and crying?" I need to avenge her death and make the murderer suffer and make his family suffer too. I need to go out there and just find that person.

"I really need to come out of the shadows and show leadership. Just know what goes around comes around!" he said with a smirk.

As he pulled out a knife and slid his tongue across the blade and then across the cheek this time causing a huge cut that spilled blood that he then drank.

Blood Spirit also turned into a cannibal from that day on because he wanted his victims to suffer more. He never really had a way of eating them but he enjoyed the heart the most.

As Blood Spirit described "It is very juicy, chewy and has a great texture to it."

He liked to rip it out of their chest. Whether they were dead or alive it was better alive because it would be fresh. Another nice bit was brain because it was chewy. Blood Spirit liked to leave the best for last. He only got to enjoy both the heart and brain on a few occasions because he would have to run instead so he wouldn't get caught by the police.

Blood Spirit had a lot of flashbacks about his mum like this but he had never cried as much. There were many cherished mementos of when they spent time together like when they were at the fun fair and they went on the Ferris wheel together. But this time, it felt unusual and remarkable because he felt as if he was in the park. As well as that, he remembered the time when she was in hospital and after school every day he went to visit her to keep her company and take care of her. But then his attention came to the day when his mum was on her deathbed.

Another day that had haunted Blood Spirit was when his dad left him. His mum and dad were never actually happy together they always used to fight because Blood Spirit's mum accused his dad of cheating. Blood Spirit's dad was actually cheating on his wife with his wife's sister, Catherine. What Blood Spirit's mum didn't know, was that it was her sister who was sleeping with her husband, later on she found out about this. When Blood Spirit found out that his dad left him, he cried all night without getting sleep and when dawn came that day he had the aim of getting control of the whole world and he wanted everyone to feel the pain of losing their family.

Chapter 13

Jealousy Kills

Location:George's house

Time: 16th July 2016

Tom was spying on Kylie for Blood Spirit to see what type of powers she had but she wasn't doing anything and he started to get bored. He sat there and waited for something to happen for several hours. He just couldn't sit there like that; he wasn't that type of person. Suddenly, his phone went off and Kylie heard. He quickly put his phone on silent and ran back but luckily his ringtone was the same as her dad's so she thought that it was just her dad's phone, so she just went back into her room again. Tom got lucky or he might have got caught by Kylie.

Tom just kept on waiting until Kylie did something. She got a piece of paper and drew on it but because it wasn't that good, she did something amazing, she crumpled up the paper and it rose up and she flicked it into the bin just using her eyes. After seeing Kylie do this Tom started to feel a bit jealous and thought if anyone found about her powers she would be popular and Tom would go back to being the one no-one cares about. Tom had to do something!

Tom looked at the time, it was nearly time to go to school so then he called up Blood Spirit and asked him to spy on Kylie because he had to go to school. Blood Spirit agreed with him and said that he would carry on spying on Kylie until he came back from school so Tom went back and Blood Spirit came. Blood Spirit decided that this was the best time for him to get Kylie's DNA so he accepted to come to spy on her or he wouldn't have even come because it would have been useless.

Blood Spirit left his hideout to go to George's house. He was excited because he wanted to know it feels to have a super-

power and he is going to have the power
of levitation. Just before he left, Tom had
told him what power Kylie had and he
never knew she had such an amazing power.
He was about to go to Kylie's house, but
Tom told him to go back because George
was going to come and stop him from going
out of the house because he saw him coming so Blood Spirit agreed. Tom was going
to go through the back way but George appeared in front of him.

George stopped Tom from getting out
of their house through the back way. "This
was what I was waiting for! I will stop you
and I will never even let you go near Kylie
"what is so special about her anyway?"

"She is special to me so I won't let you
take her!" said George.

"Well if you are going to get in my way

then I will have to take you down, but I can't do it now and I won't tell you why I can't!" said Blood Spirit. So then he ran away and escaped but George didn't chase him because he was fine if he was gone but as long as Kylie was still there he was fine. Just who was he?

Once George was sure that Tom had gone, he rushed to Kylie's room to check on her and made she was still there. He was relieved that she was still there but he was still worried for her because Tom was gone for long and he would come back for her so he needed to protect her with all power he has. Blood Spirit would be George's hardest enemy to face by far. It kept worrying him of how he would keep Kylie safe she is somewhat...mysterious? There is something she has that Blood Spirit wants and he need to find out what it is.

Kylie was sitting in her room. She had noticed that her father had popped up near her room and he had a worried look on his face, it was shocking! I had never seen him like that before. He was mostly cheerful but only sometimes he was stressed out but that's all I have seen of him before but today he had a different look on his face. I don't know what happened to him but all I know is that there is something going on that I don't know. I looked for him but I couldn't find him.

George was down at the MI5 headquarters trying to find more information about Blood Spirit. He had done something very clever he had placed a chip on his shoulder, which was a tracking device so he could see where Tom was going and he could find out where their hideout was. Suddenly, his tracking device stopped and didn't go anywhere for another 15 minutes so then George figured out that Tom had found the tracking device and had had dropped it somewhere. His amazing plan had been ruined he had a chance to find their hideout and he had failed.

George just forgot that all of it happened, he went back up to doing his normal thing, to earn money; selling baked potatoes. He wasn't upset anymore or worried, he was back to normal as he always is. Then Kylie came into the room and she said "Hi George, where did you go? I tried to look for you and I couldn't find you anywhere?"

"Oh, I just went out to get something for us to eat."

"Oh, Ok" said Kylie.

George started peeling potatoes and Kylie came over to help "Thanks." he said.

"No problem." Kylie said.

George was doing his work as normal when he got a phone call from his boss Rizwan and he said "Hi, George I've heard there's some guy called Blood Spirit and he is after the kid that you took from Dean Orphanage, is this true?"

"Yes, boss this is true and I am definitely NOT sending my child back to the orphanage she is my child now and I won't let Blood Spirit past me to get her. I don't know why he is after her but I have to stop him." George explained.

"Thanks for informing me, George."

His boss Rizwan said. "Bye." And he put the phone down.

Chapter 14

Deceitful Thinking

Location: under Edinburgh Castle

Time: 6th July 2016

Flashback

"So I want you to kill both Kylie and Audrey, they have had enough attention in their lives. They are always the main ones. What about poor old me? I don't think it's acceptable that I don't get any attention. I want to be different too. I'm not just being a bad friend, if they were true friends they won't mind if they die for me" said Tom. Tom made sure no one was listening to him. For a few seconds he thought he was doing something wrong but nodded his head and thought that whatever he was doing was right and was for his happiness.

"Ok, ok, I will do your work but what's in it for me?" said Blood Spirit.

"You obviously know that I won't disappoint you, I will give you some of the DNA from Kylie, which will help you in

your future assassinations. You can become telepathic." said Tom.

"Kylie is the person whose DNA you
needed two years ago but you couldn't get.
Remember the day we went to the hospital?" Blood Spirit was intrigued and said
yes. Blood Spirit was already looking for
Kylie's DNA since two years when Tom
and Blood Spirit first met and Blood Spirit
helped Tom to fake his illness.

"So, " Tom explained

"Blood Spirit, I want you to do a job
for me."

"Yes of course." Blood Spirit said, confused "but what do you want me to do?"

"I want you to kill Audrey and Kylie, I
want them DEAD, you understand? DEAD!
Will you be the man for this job?"

"Yes, I won't let you down." He replied

calmly with a sly look on his face.

"I hope not." grinned Tom with a venomous glint in his eyes.

Chapter 15

Deadly Influences

Location:Tom's house

Time: 18th July 2016

Audrey picked up his phone and wrote

down Tom's number. Audrey was feeling nervous; his palms were sweating. He called Tom for advice on his decision on committing suicide. He was the last friend he had to ask for advice. Audrey's mind told him that it was the right decision. But he wanted some reassurance before ending his own life.

"Hello Audrey!" said an excited Tom.

"Hi, why are you so excited?" said Audrey.

"You called me of course! My best friend! I haven't heard from you in a long time that's all."

"It's good to hear from you too. But I called you to ask a question."

"Ask away Audrey." said Tom curiously.

"The thing is, you know how I have

bipolar disorder." said Audrey anxiously.

"Of course and I'm always here if you need me."

"Due to my disorder, my parents left me when I was fifteen, as soon as my sister left to become a lawyer. Also, since I've had a rough time lately, I was thinking of committing suicide. Plus, I have had suicidal thoughts lately and attempted to commit suicide multiple times."

At that moment, Tom was happier than he had ever been. He didn't have to do anything for his plan to work. He tried his hardest to not show his happiness.

"Well, I hate to say this to you, but if you don't want to live with yourself then you should commit suicide." Tom said with suppressed grin.

"The thing is, if I was in your shoes I

would do it. There is no point of living a
life that you hate and don't want to live.
Plus I'm sure God would give you a better life in the next one. You would obviously go through nothing than go through
everything bad in life?" said a rather excited Tom. "Well those are all true points.
I knew you would give me good advice.
That's why I called you." said a sad and
depressed Audrey.

A million thoughts were going through
Audrey's head. He was thinking about his
sister Faith but also about Tom's advice.

"Audrey, if you know you are going to
go through more pain if you live then you're
better of committing suicide." said Tom.

"I don't know now, maybe things can
change. My sister said to remember that
if anything bad happens something good

always comes out of it." replied Audrey.

At that moment, Tom started to panic a little. He knew if he didn't try harder to persuade Audrey to commit suicide then his plan would fail.

There was an eerie, awkward silence on the line. Tom was thinking hard about what to say next to say to Audrey.

"I'm sure your parents left you because they didn't want to see you go through any pain. At least they would come to your funeral. You will make your parents happy. They never wanted to see you go through any pain. That's why they left you. If you want to do something do it. You will always get another chance. You are special in my eyes. Committing suicide will benefit you. Think about you before you think about others." Tom said.

"I don't want to go through any more pain. I guess my parents did want the best for me." said Audrey.

"I'm sure everyone would understand your decision. You know you didn't want to live with yourself, you didn't want to suffer any more pain, you just want to make your parent's wishes come true, so you'll obviously get a second chance. You don't need to worry just do it." said Tom.

"Thank you so much! I appreciate your help and advice." said Audrey.

He instantly ended the call after that.

Audrey dropped the phone on the table. He knew what he had to do next. First he took time to reminisce about his life. He remembered what his sister had said. "Anything bad that happens something good always comes out of it." But he knew that wouldn't help now. He had set his mind on committing suicide. No one was going to stop him. He had been waiting for this moment for a long time. He was home alone. No social workers were around. No Faith was around. Now all he had to do was get the rope.

Chapter 16

Suspections And Suicide

Location:Royal Edinburgh Hospital

Time: 20th July 2016

Audrey was wondering whether what

he was doing the right thing. Should he commit suicide? To double check if he was making the right decision...he called Kylie and had a long conversation that lasted all the way until tea time. Kylie was surprised by all of this and couldn't believe that Tom would do such a thing and would convince Audrey to do suicide. Kylie told Audrey that doing suicide was wrong and he should never do that as it is harmful for his body. After 15 minutes of explaining and lecturing Audrey to why he shouldn't suicide, he finally gave in and put his rope away.

As well as talking about that, Audrey told Kylie that he had suspicions on Tom as he thought Tom was spying on Kylie. Kylie found this hard to believe as she thought Tom couldn't spy on her. He's

not a stalker. He wouldn't sit in a car outside her house with binoculars and looking
at her every move. However, than Kylie
started remembering all the times she had
seen Tom near or around her, and that
maybe that was not a coincidence and Tom
might have been following her. One thought
was spinning in Kylie's head...he's my friend...so
why would he stalk me?

Kylie locked all her windows, doors and
closed the curtains, so Tom wouldn't be
able to see her and as she was doing that,
she realised that the car that had been
parked outside her house was really Tom's
car. The blue range rover had been parked
outside her house for nearly a month and
she swore she saw someone in there every day but then realised maybe it was her
mind playing tricks on her. Kylie was un-

sure of all this and as she was closing her last window, she shivered a little.

After being so paranoid that he was outside, Kylie walked out of her house with a pocket knife, to get a bar of chocolate from her local corner shop. She saw Tom with a mysterious guy in a black suit. She thought it may have been a relative of some sort but as she had a knife, she wasn't scared. She could use the pocket knife as self-protection in case Tom and the guy in the suit tried to do anything to her. But seeing as Tom was one of her friends, she doubted that he'd tried to hurt her, however she didn't say hello to him when she walked out of her house.

Whilst buying her Chocolate bar, she started getting very anxious as no one would be home and Tom along with his unknown relative might break in and snoop around in her house, steal things and make a mess. Furthermore, Kylie remembered a conversation she had with Tom when he mentioned him being a multiple young offender for stealing many electronics, money from the bank and not paying for food from a restaurant and walking out. After remembering this conversation, it made Kylie even more concerned as to what Tom is capable of doing.

Kylie wanted to spy on Tom.

"Two can play at that game!" said Kylie to herself.

Kylie went to Tom's house and looked inside the window through binoculars but there was nothing doubtful or suspicious that was happening...Tom was just eating dinner with his mum. Kylie wondered where his dad.

She muttered to herself, "This is just a big waste of time, if he did spy on me, he's not doing it now, " and with that Kylie went back home where George was waiting for her with her dinner.

It was fish and chips and for dessert they had some pudding.

"Where were you?" asked George as it was 8pm at night, the latest Kylie had ever come home. "At Tom's house, I didn't keep a track of time." She said.

"Ok, but if you are going to a friend's house tell me first, these days there a lot of bad people out on the streets."

Kylie nodded carelessly and went upstairs to her room.

Chapter 17

An Unknown Agent

```
Location:George's house

Time: 22nd July 2016
```

Kylie suspected that Tom was faking

his mental health illness and she was determined to find out what actually happened and why Tom lied about his illness. Kylie had a cunning plan to reveal whether Tom's illness was real or fake. She was really confused but then she thought about it and knew exactly who to call. The number 1 agent from the top agency: it was Katie. She dialed her number, 07945312280, a lady picked up.

"This is your client wanting to meet you at The Newington Coffee Shop tomorrow at 12pm, there is a mission that needs to be completed...URGENTLY!" Kylie said.

She ended the call before the lady had a chance to speak. Kylie took a deep breath and waited until tomorrow.

As the next day arrived, time was ticking and it was already 11:21am. Kylie got ready to meet Katie. Katie went in her jet black Mercedes and drove off to the Coffee Shop in town and Kylie went to the coffee shop in a taxi. After 13 minutes, Katie arrived. Kylie was already there waiting for her. As they started a conversation a waitress came over but turned back as soon as she saw that Katie was an agent.

"So, what was so urgent Kylie?", Katie asked.

"I have a very important mission for you that needs to be solved immediately". Kylie told Katie.

"There is someone who I have my suspicions about." Kylie said.

"Who?" Replied Katie

"His name is Tom and I think he may be faking that he has anxiety. I think he just self-harms himself to gain attention or something like that. Your job now, is to pretend to be his fake sister so that you can get closer to him and that you just came out of prison, that is why Tom has never seen you before as he was only 4 years old. If he asks why you went to jail, say it was because your ex- best friend had tortured you, therefore you had killed her. Make sure you do the job properly, I need this mission to be successful."

Katie sighs, to herself and thought to herself,

"If I am doing this job for Kylie what am I getting in return?"

As Katie agreed to this mission, she asked Kylie what she would get in return.

"Well, if this mission is a success, you're likely to get a promotion for doing such a great job as well as that, that will be very good for your career". Kylie responded

"I will make sure that you never get employed as an agent ever again in your life.I know it sounds quite drastic, however you don't understand my situation...It is very, very serious."

A few minutes later, Katie drove off in her car. She had agreed to this mission even though it was going to be very hard for her to complete it. She took a deep breath and looked through the window as she drove off back to her house. As she parked her car in the driveway, she went inside and called for a taxi, while she packed her clothes and went over of what she was going to say to Tom. As the taxi arrived outside the house, Katie looked back one more time and then she sat in the taxi.

As she sat in the taxi, she thought, what a cruel agent she could be at times. But she knew it was for a good cause, because she was going to be promoted, but the worst thing was that she was worried about getting caught and being sent to jail. After seven minutes, Katie had finally arrived at Tom's house. She paused for a moment as she thought how Tom would look like and react. Katie then sighed and rang the doorbell.

"Ring, ring".

The doorbell made a weird squeaky noise as Katie heard a low voice from inside saying:

"I'll get it." said Tom

Chapter 18

Abuse

```
Location:Tom's house

Time: 24th July 2016
```

Tom heard a knock on his door. He stood up worried and wondered who might it be.The knock came again so Tom went and opened the door and to his surprise, he found a girl with a suitcase standing there. She looked as if she hadn't had a bath in weeks and hadn't eaten recently.

"May I help you?" he asked.

"I am Katie and I need to speak with you about something. To make a long story short, let me in and I'll tell me everything" replied Katie.

Tom let Katie in the house and she was welcomed into his lounge with a cup of tea and some biscuits. He politely asked her some questions and was gobsmacked and found out that she was his sister. He found out that she had committed a crime because her ex best friend had tortured her. Tom felt insecure about being around her as she had murdered someone. However then Tom thought about what he was go-

ing to do to ignore it. After a bit, Tom
believed that she was his sister as she was
exactly like him and they shared a lot in
common. Later on, they changed the sub-
ject and started to talk about everyday life
and what any normal brother and sister
would talk about.

"Anyways, what's that noise?" exclaimed
Katie,

"It's probably mum and dad shouting
as usual." Tom said grumpily.

"No, it seems unusual, let's go see, "
said Katie in a scared voice.

The pair ran upstairs as fast as they
could to see what was happening and why
there was so much noise. After they opened
the creaky door, Katie was shocked to have
seen such a catastrophic moment. They
entered the dull room, perceiving every-

thing around them.

Katie was astonished to see that Tom's dad was abusing his mum; pushing her around the room, punching her, slapping her as if she were a toy, it was a horrific sight!

Shouting at the top of her voice, mum cried, Why are you doing this to me? What have I ever done to you to deserve this?'

Her face and arms were shadowed with bruises and cuts.

"You have made my life a misery and now I'm getting payback!' exclaimed dad.

Simultaneously, worried Tom and Katie were sitting in the corner of the tedious room, pondering what would happen next.

Out of nowhere, John chucked a glass vase at Basima but ended up hitting Tom and Katie.Crying their eyes out, they ran to their mum, hoping she would comfort them and make them safe. Dad obviously didn't care that he hit the kids and ran off, leaving mum to care for the kids.

Who are you?' Mum was staring at Katie and wondering who on earth she could be!?

Katie was worried but still explained everything fluently to mum and surprisingly mum believed everything and gave both children a big hug. They all knew this was a moment never to be forgotten. Mum thought to herself, why are such innocent children, experiencing such sinister drama. She told them to go upstairs while she cleared up. While clearing up, she noticed that one family picture, which had many sentimental values, had been shattered into pieces. She burst into tears

and prayed that everything would soon get
better.

A few hours after John came home, Basima
was waiting in the living room and the kids
were upstairs sleeping. In a calm voice,
mum spoke to dad and said that she wanted
to separate from him. Dad agreed to this
decision but wanted the kids to stay with
him. However, mum also wanted the kids
to stay with her. As a result, another dis-
pute took place and mum had had enough.
She kicked him out the house until he was
ready to treat her with care. After all the
loud shouting, Katie eventually woke up
and mum and her had a talk about how
life was without her being around.

Chapter 19

Hello Police, Bye Dad

```
Location: Tom's house

Time: 26th July 2016
```

That next morning, Katie and Tom suddenly woke up due to the loud noise and arguing. Katie had enough of all this drama; she was on a mission to frame Tom but in the process she had realised that her stepdad for the mission was abusing Basima really badly. Who would have thought she would sabotage her own family? They both couldn't sleep properly due to all the commotion, which had occurred and it was on their mind that whole night. Tom wanted them to be a normal family with no problems and wanted to have a good life. He wished for everything to be okay and for everyone to have a good relationship with each other. But he knew it would never happen, it was just his imagination that was playing tricks on him.

Katie secretly crept downstairs and hid behind the door and recorded all the arguing and abuse. She knew that if she had shown this to someone, their whole family would be over, but did she want that to happen or not? She recorded every single detail from where they started talking to when it escalated to hitting. Katie knew she had to do something to stop them fighting...and she knew she had to take this step forward. The only thing she could do now was record them and show it to Kylie. Kylie would know what to do and would approach this situation properly. Katie ducked behind the sofa as she heard a noise near her. She realised that it was just the wind and ran back upstairs with the evidence in her hand. She watched the video one more time to make sure that she was doing the right thing. She sighed and lay back in her bed. As she made a call to Kylie, she was worried about getting caught and her mission would not come successful as Tom would hate her for putting his step-dad in jail and breaking up their family.

"Hi Katie. How can I help you?" Kylie asked.

"I have got footage of John abusing Basima. This is my chance to put John in prison. What do you think I should do?" Katie answered

"Well I think I should call the police for you so you don't get caught and you keep concentrating on the mission that I told you to do."

"Thanks Kylie!" Said Katie, before hanging up.

A few minutes later, Kylie rang up the police and reported John for abusive behaviour.

"We need the police to be sent down to 21 Sheriff Park EH6 0PD as soon as possible, as a woman, aged 45, is being abused by her husband who's aged 52." Katie Said.

She exaggerated immensely by saying there were kids in the house and they were also beaten. She thought this was the right idea and perfect moment for dad to have been taken away and never come back.

Katie's heart was beating fast as the doorbell rang, she knew it was too late to go back, so she ran downstairs pretending that she had done nothing wrong.

They didn't stop knocking until somebody opened the door. Mum opened it with a bright red, crying face, and the police stormed in.

They went to John and said "I'm arresting you for abusing your family members and being violent to other citizens, anything you say will be given as evidence in court."

Vigorously, he tried to escape and push the policemen but it was no use for him. In the corner of the room, Katie was smirking and laughing; she had accomplished her mission. Whereas, Tom was startled and was speculated to know who would have incapacitated their family. Mum felt relieved that she was now in a safe environment and her kids were with her, but felt bewildered as she didn't know how the police found out about this.

John was very frustrated, he looked back at Basima and gave her a look that she could never forget. John was devastated of what he just did and how he hurt his family, he wanted to put it right but it was too late for that.

A few minutes later they had arrived at the police station. As he got out of the car, John started to act aggressive towards the policeman. The policeman dragged John and put him in a cell. John thrust his head in his hands as the police started coming into his cell. It was interview time. He recorded everything which was being said.

"Here present today Detective Chief Inspector (DCI) Matt Phillips and Police Constable (PC) Stacy Smith and John the culprit. Now John, why have you been abusing your wife and your children?"

" I haven't done anything, it's my wife, she got into a fight with some other people and came crying home, and do you really think I'll beat up my children, I'm not the kind of man to do this." Replied John.

"Well you have no evidence to prove your point so your court hearing will be in approximately three weeks due to the jury being away, and you will be kept in a police cell for the night, that is it for now."

John puts his hands in a fist and swings for the the DCI Matt but he missed and fell on the floor.

"This is not my fault at all, you lot will pay for this!".

Chapter 20

Mysterious Hackers

Location:The Baked Potatoes Shop,

Time: 28th July 2016

"Kylie! Are you ready for school? I am

late to go to work." George said.

George was getting calls from the MI5, Blood Spirit was causing mass destruction in Edinburgh, trying to get George's location but the MI5 secured George's house so signal can come in but it cannot leave. And the reason MI5 fitted a satellite phone inside an IPhone was so Kylie could call her friends but Blood Spirit can't track Kylie's signal. Kylie rushed down the stairs because she was late for school and Kylie and George sat in their Ford Fiesta and George dropped her to school and he went to work.

George entered The Baked Potatoes Shop and went down to the MI5 headquarters.He looked around the MI5 HQ and saw that everyone's faces were full with stress and worry. He went to Jeffrey.

"What's with the dull faces" he asked.

"It's Blood Spirit He killed the Chief's family, looking for you, but the Chief still didn't give your location."replied

With rage and fury George went to his cabin and opened his Laptop, he looked at CCTV footage to see where Blood Spirit went after the murder of the Chief's family.He looked at the footage but he never found where Blood Spirit went afterwards.

George was stressing out because it was his fault that the Chief lost his family.Suddenly, an email came from Blood Spirit.It read

"Dear George,

You must be wondering how I got your email but don't worry, this is just the start.Next I will find your house and destroy it with you in it.But if you give me Kylie NOW! I'll play easy on you and you won't suffer but if you don't you will suffer like the Chiefs family and like the rest of Edinburgh which is going to destroyed

I am coming for you.

Just be ready.

Blood Spirit"

George was freaking out. He was afraid that this was going to be his first failed mission because he couldn't track Blood Spirit and he was slowly getting closer to him. He thought that he did not deserve this mission and he will let the Chief down but then he remembered the email, it was electronic so using the MI5 hacking team he could find the location of where the email came from. Blood Spirit wouldn't send it in public so he may of sent it from somewhere private and this may give him the location of Blood Spirits lair or where he was headed to.

George went towards the chiefs office, half way there, he trips with the computer which contains the location of Blood Spirit. The data was gone but he still had the original email and he sent it back to the hacking team for the location. After it was complete he went to the chief to get permission to fight Blood Spirit after he was found. The Chief still in a bad mood after the death of his family, "Yes." The Chief said.

George tried to comfort him and tried to feel his sorrow but he said he needed some time alone.

George got his weapons ready.He wore a bulletproof vest and some black gloves.He made a whole bag full of lethal weapons and was ready to go, he was waiting for the location but then Jeffrey and some other agents approached George.

"George you can't go alone, we are coming with you." They said

"That is not possible, sorry!" replied George

"We are not taking no for an answer."

"Ok guys, but you could only come in if... I send a signal!"

"Fine! But if we think anything is getting out of control we are coming in."

"You are under my command over there! Ok!"

"Ok!"

"George! George!" a voice came from the hacking team.

George sprinted to the ward where hacking was being done.

"George! He is on the move.Look! This

location has changed and he is going somewhere now."

George looked at the map and it looked
like Blood Spirit found out where Kylie
studied.George was freaking out, he couldn't
understand how Blood Spirit was getting
to know all the places where George and
Kylie go.This could seriously get everyone
in trouble.George said to the backup team
that they have to leave.

George got out the MI5 HQ, he told
the backup crew to take the helicopter to
the school until they caught up with Blood
Spirit and distracts him so he couldn't reach
Kylies school in time.George got into his
Maserati and he sped down the streets of
Edinburgh to the motorway.He took the
M8 so he could reach Blood Spirit as soon
as possible. He wasn't sure if he was go-

ing to make it. Then to make things even worse the backup team called and said the helicopter is already taken to mission and that they are in there in a car going to the school.

George didn't want to lose Kylie, he couldn't put Kylie's life at risk so he called the school.

"Hello, This is De." The school receptionist answered

"I CAN'T TALK RIGHT NOW BUT LISTEN TO ME CAREFULLY, OK! I AM FROM THE MI5 AND I WANT YOU TO TAKE KYLIE TO THE NEAREST SUPERMARKET BUT DON'T GO THROUGH THE MAIN STREETS AND I DON'T WANT YOU TO GET SPOTTED! DO YOU UNDERSTAND! GIVE ME YOUR NUMBER JUST IN-CASE I NEED TO CALL YOU!" Georg got the number but was stressed out.Instead of following Blood Spirit he went to the supermarket where Kylie was going to be dropped off.

On the way, George saw Blood Spirit, Blood Spirit wasn't taking the main road to the school but the road where Kylie and her teacher were supposed to come from.He called the teacher just in time so they could hide somewhere and Blood Spirit did not see them.George told them to come to the main road and he waited for her there.Then finally George saw Kylie and he took her to his house.

Chapter 21

Insert title here

Location:At the park, At faith's house

Time: 30th July 2016

Faith continuously thought about the flashback where Audrey tried to commit suicide. He tried to give up his life. He was sick. He needed help. He didn't trust anyone. She felt wounded that she hadn't been the big sister that anyone would have ever wanted. She still couldn't believe her younger brother wanted to give up his life, because he couldn't overcome a disease and had no belief in himself and the amazing creative boy inside him.

"Why! Why Audrey! Why not me!! What has Audrey ever done!!! He's only ever helped people! He's true from heart!!" Faith shrieked.

She ran to the park, feeling insane. She didn't know what to do. She sat on a bench still crying.

"Mum mum mum, can we go on a picnic tomorrow as well!" a little girl cried.

She looked so happy, enjoying her biscuits and sandwich with her family.

" No no dear, your daddy needs to go to Glasgow tomorrow, you know your cousin Amy? She has a Bipolar disorder, daddy is going to a lab tomorrow to get a cure!" the mother warmly said to her daughter smiling.

An idea struck Faith's mind like lightning! It was the perfect idea! She knew this was perfect and maybe could save and bring back her little brother from the clutches of no self control.

She ran back home, running as fast as the wind, like a lion in a race, this was a race, a race of the love of a sister. She slammed the door behind her as she saw Audrey sitting watching tv, eyes red and sore with tears. She stopped and looked at her brother, she took a long think and thought about him. She was determined and made a final decision. She knew exactly what she had to do.

Faith went up to her crisp bedroom and packed all her valuables that she needed on her journey and logged onto her computer. In a few clicks she booked a seat in Railways Trains to Glasgow. She breathed, she knew this was the only way. She wanted her brother more than anything, and this was her chance to prove she was a good big sister!

Faith searched more and more and more about her brother's mental illness - Bipolar Disorder. She searched and searched, tab after tab, browsing all night, and finally, before her eyes almost shut due to lack of sleep, she clicked onto a website which only showed one address = Lab of Labs, The Doctors Dome - Glasgow. There was a blurred image of how the Lab looked like. It was a big dome shape and blue with glass crystals. Everything looked so fancy yet serious. The place looked like as if it did not even exist.

"Yes!" she exclaimed.

Her sleep and tiredness ripping off her heart once she found a solution, hoping. She hoped to have found what she was looking, and in her lucky stars, she was right. She found a website showing the exact location where a cure was being made for Bipolar disease that could fix her brother. She continued reading more and more and found much more detail on it, however she found due to the rareness of the cure being found, if the scientists chose to sell it, it would cost more than someone's profit in a lifetime. She was determined to help her brother and prove her love for him, and she knew this was the perfect way.

Faith grabbed her luggage and looked back at the house she just arrived at a few weeks ago after several years. Once again she had to leave to fulfil something she believed in, and she felt torn. She didn't want to leave, but she had to do this, her name wasn't just a word. She had faith that her little brother would get cured, her heart just knew it, but her mind told her to stay and support her brother, not to leave him alone again. She thought about her decision once again. Was it wrong to leave her brother and put him in the pain again? But she wanted to fix him and wanted her real brother back more than anything. Her heart told her to go, go out on a quest to find a cure to bring back her sibling, and listening to the heart is the wisest thing.

Chapter 22

Masterminds

Location:Under Edinburgh castle in Blood Spi

Time: 2nd August 2016

Blood Spirit was stood tall, looking down
on his minions, who were all gathered for
another meeting with their master.Blood

Spirit was gave the brief of their mission to kill Kylie.

"Listen up! You have got one job today and one job only! It is to kill Kylie and remember don't come back if she is not dead or you will be dead!" Blood Spirit told them with anger shown on his face.

All the minions replied "Yes master".

They all knew not to object their master because the consciences were just brutal. First Blood Spirit would start chewing then he would go onto pulling the heart out of chest while his victim was still alive. Blood Spirit's minions know this because it is done in front of everyone. This has only happened to three people Kevin, Stuart and Bob. No one has ever dared to object again.

"Now I know how stupid some of you

can be so I am going to show you a picture of her" Blood Spirit said holding up a picture of Kylie.

Then he passed it to his minions and they passed it to each other and one by one they all saw it and on all of their faces a slight smirk started to appear.

"Understand now! No mistakes should occur or you know what's going to happen. He pulled out a knife and slid his tongue across the blade and then across his cheek causing a huge cut again in the same place and again it spilled blood that he again devoured. They all gulped as the disturbing images came to them.

"Now rise from the shadows and attack!" Blood Spirit shouted.

"GO GO GO!" Blood Spirit screeched at his minions.

His voice piercing through the air like a fighter jet. His minions all ran out the door and straight to Kylie after they found out where she was. Within a few minutes of travelling, they reached their destination and standing in front of them was Kylie, who was confounded of what was happening.

"What's going on?" she staggeringly asked.

Mark replied, "We were sent here to put you to sleep forever!"

After hearing this, Kylie's eyes opened so wide as she was gobsmacked.

She had no idea of what was going on and what was going to happen.

"Why are you doing this?" Kylie asked.

"We were told to come here by our master and your worst nightmare" replied one of the minions.

They held Kylie's arm and tried with all their strength to take her. She was resisting. The minions were now getting annoyed. Then one of them pulled out a gun and Kylie stopped and turned back. Click went the gun. Her heart was racing.

"Who is your master?" asked Kylie

"Blood Spirit" replied a different minion.

"Why is he doing this" asked Kylie.

"Ask him yourself when we get there" replied the same minion.

"But before we go let us welcome you to our way" said another minion.

Suddenly, they all started throwing punches at her. Kylie fell to the ground with a shriek. Luckily for her George heard and was coming but he still had to get a pistol from his car which was around the corner, he sped off to get his pistol. Meanwhile all of the minions now we're joining in kicking the poor girl who was on the floor moaning. George was just around the corner now.

"Oi! Stop!" shouted George.

All the minions turned and looked at him with a big smile.

George got in the way of the minions and saved Kylie from them. He rapidly whipped his gun out and started to shoot at the minions. If it wasn't for George Kylie would be on her deathbed. Minions scurried away like ants. There were dead bodies everywhere. Kylie was safe but severely injured.

"Boss that MI5 agent got in the way and saved Kylie. Our plan was foiled. We don't know what to do next to get Kylie." said one of the minions.

"Well you should've done your job properly then. I don't care what it takes but you have to do whatever it takes to kill her. Even if you have to kill George then do it. But we need those powers from Kylie no matter what." said Bloodspirit. Blood Spirit was now getting frustrated.

"Which powers! Boss?"

"TELEKINESIS! Actually don't worry about George. I'll take care of him myself."

George was in Blood Spirits way to get to Kylie. He was as angry as a wasps, whose hive had been attacked. George was the only obstacle in the way of his perfect plan. But he was determined to change that as soon as he met face to face with

George. His face was as red as fire. Blood Spirit was livid. If it wasn't for this MI5 agent his life would be smooth. But he learnt that nothing goes how he wants it to go. At least he was going to make sure that everything ran smoothly after their encounter.

There they stood, both in the middle of the rusty, ancient cellar, with the tension rising up in the atmosphere. Immediately, they both reached for their inner pocket. George then pulled out a small pistol from his back pocket, however Blood spirit, pulled out his special dagger, the one which was dripping with blood. He threw his knife away and said

"Let's fight like men; the proper way without weapons." Said Blood Spirit.

Just then, George chucked his pistol across

the room and agreed. Blood spirit made
the first move and punched George on his
face, leaving a black patch near his eye.
George got furious and pushed him into
the wall and continuously slapped him until he got red marks on his face. After a
few minutes of fighting, George had no energy within himself and gave up fighting.

There he was, George was lying on the
floor, half beaten to death. He had now
known not to ever mess with Blood Spirit
and really regretted it.Then Blood Spirit
got out another dagger and cut Georges
leg. Blood was dripping down from his
leg had a very deep cut in his leg.; he has
bruises all over his arms as if he got beaten
with a cricket bat; he had a black patch on
his eye; his clothes were full of blood and
where all ripped and ragged. Whereas,

Blood Spirit was laughing menacingly as he had finally beaten up George. He was proud for what he had done to him and let him to rot on the floor in his prison cell.

Chapter 23

The Fatal Injury

Location:Royal Edinburgh Hospital

Time: 4th August 2016

George was severely injured as Blood
Spirit took a dagger and stabbed George
along his calf muscle. He was in agony

and pain but he still fought the pain and managed to still get up he needed help and was dizzy, he didn't know what to do. He thought that in any moment he could faint and die on the spot but he thought about Kylie and managed to restrain his strength. He was thinking of what he could do to get help but he was in way too much pain and shock to do anything.

Suddenly an idea came to him, he could use his watch to call the MI5 headquarters so they could help him and get him to safety! He called his boss Rizwan.Rizwan picked the phone

"Hi, George what's up?" He George

"I'm dying here please send h...help p-please.!"

"Ok don't worry I will send reinforcements." Rizwan Said.

"Thanks b-boss." exclaimed George.

And with that he collapsed to the ground with no strength in his body left. The reinforcements started to come in and they came to the aid of George, they called in the medic's to help up George and perform an operation on George's leg.

In a turn of events, George uses his watch and sends the SOS signal to the backup team because his first call was interrupted.Fighting the pain he stood up and told Blood Spirit and his Minion that this the end of them.Blood spirit heard the sounds of the sirens from the helicopters and the bullet proof MI5 cars, he started to go ballistic.He went to George and said that this isn't the last he will hear of him. Promptly he turned and told his minions to leave but in that time the MI5 had arrived.

Throughout the maniac, George's vision was going blurry.he was laying on the floor trying to move but he couldn't but he saw a figure but could not make out who it was.Then he said "George, George, George" The voice echoed in George's ears getting fainter and fainter " it's, it's, it's. Me, Me, Me. Jeffrey, Jeffrey, Jeffrey." He picked George up and took him to the helicopter ambulance. George wasn't feeling well and the wound was very deep.The MI5 hurried to the Hospital trying to reach in time so George doesn't lose his life.

"H-Hi Kylie." said George.

"Dad! Thank God you're okay! Why are you so hurt?! What happened?" Said Kylie.

"Oh, Kylie I have been hiding so many

things from you I'm so sorry!" said George.

"I'm an agent who works for the MI5 and the headquarters is right underneath our baked potato shop!"

"I only adopted you because Blood Spirit was after you! But it doesn't mean I don't like you as a daughter."

"I'm so sorry that I hid all of this from you!" explained George.

"This was all a mission, but adopting you wasn't part of it please believe me.

"If I survive then I will stay with you until I die because you are my daughter." Said George.

"Oh dad! I will never leave you too." Exclaimed Kylie.

On the way to the hospital George was getting worse and worse and Kylie was very worried for him. She hoped that everything would go right and George would go back to normal. Even though George said that he didn't get Kylie by his own choice she didn't mind because now she thinks of her as his own daughter and that was fine by Kylie because if George didn't come to the orphanage she would have been all alone without a father.

They were really close to the hospital when the driver smashed into something. When Kylie looked back she saw that the driver had smashed the traffic lights and just carried on driving.

"We bribed the driver to take me to the hospital really quickly or we would kill him as we are the MI5, so now he is scared so he is driving quickly and also way over the speed limit and now he doesn't care what he hits into, his main is to take me to the hospital. Both of them laughed happily and were joyful only for a minute because pain started surging through George and he stopped laughing.

George had got to the hospital and they got off and ran in when suddenly, his watch started ringing. He was getting a call from one of the agents.

"George a-all of us have been taken down, he is too s-strong for us I think now he is coming a-after you so watch out!" Said an agent "All of us are injured and some are dead this is a big problem, if you want to you call some more reinforcements because some of them are still at headquarters." The agent explained.

"There's no need for that, I don't want more of our agents to die I can handle this. Thank you for informing me." said George sympathetically.

George told Kylie that she needed to go somewhere safe because she was that one that Blood Spirit wanted but he couldn't think of anywhere he could take her to. Then an idea popped into his head.

"Kylie a helicopter is going to come and take you somewhere safe and don't ask me where you are going, all you need to know is that you will be safe there." George explained.

"Ok, dad I trust you." George went on his watch and called the headquarters

"Bring a helicopter to Royal Edinburgh hospital quickly!" shouted George.

"Yes, sir!" said the agent.

The helicopter came really quickly and George spoke to the agents and told them to take Kylie to any safe house and keep her safe. Before Kylie went George told her to stay safe and if anything happens he told her to stay with the agents before they were fully qualified and professional agents so they both said their bye's and Kylie got onto the helicopter and left with the agents. Now George was alone and he had to think up of something to stop Blood Spirit from doing his evil deeds. He was still especially worried for Kylie but he was sure the agents could take care of her.

Chapter 24

The Evil Is Victorious

Location:MI5 hideout, Blood Spirit's hideo

Time: 6th August 2016

"Go agents! Bring me back suitable ev-

idence or even Blood spirits body! I need
to get rid of this evil master-mind and save
Edinburgh from his evil reign. I also need
to save Kylie from him!" boomed George-
his echo blaring all over the room.

"Just do my job right, or their would be
serious consequences, you will see a totally
different side of me, lads." hissed George.

The agents sighed, they knew it was a
hard mission to be solved and make Edinburgh safe, but they heard George, their
would be consequences.

The MI5 went to Blood spirit's secret
hide-out and hid under cover. Soon, they
gathered their courage and confidence and
went up to fight Blood spirit. They all
fought for what they believe in and continued no matter what. They stood opposite Blood spirit, perhaps facing their ul-

timate death. They all prayed that their fight for truth would succeed, and they all believed and vowed to try their hardest. They looked at Blood Spirit straight in his eyes and felt the vibe that they had to put their full energy in this. Blood Spirit and his powers were too defeatable against the agents of MI5.

Sadly, the truth was defeated and evil reigned. Blood Spirit killed the MI5 agents. Their bodies were crumpled on the floor; blood scattered everywhere, it was horrific. But the fight wasn't over yet, it was still in their hearts, their vow, Blood Spirit will die.

"Mwahahahahahaha!" he cackled evilly.

"CHOMP!"

Blood Spirit took a big crunchy bite out of one of the agents.

"Mmmmm, I love human flesh!"

He licked his dry lips and took a few more juicy bites. Yet he did not notice that they were still alive. Blood dripping everywhere on the floor, he licked the blood off the floor with pleasure. He laughed "Mwhahahahaha!", he was happy enough that he defeated MI5 and he now rules Edinburgh.

"Right, now I need to get rid of these bodies, well, bodies with bits of flesh and half bits in my tummy hahah!"

He quickly hid the bodies and ran towards the big river that was near his hideout. He dumped all of the MI5 agent's bodies. Their lives completely ended right there, sunken in water, with bite marks on their necks, nobody would suspect a thing.

"Ahhh! My minions! My poor minions!

You sacrificed your lives just for me! I shall get my revenge." he angrily promised.

Yet, he did not know that promises aren't made from the mind, they are made from the heart, truthfully from the heart. His minions died for him to have the reign of Edinburgh.

Blood Spirit ran away rapidly from the crime scene so that he could continue his evil plans and succeed on his mission! He carefully made sure he left no clues so he wouldn't get caught. He felt unstoppable and powerful, however, he did not know he was living in a lie. As he went back to his hideout he covered up the tracks of his footprints.

As he continued walking down the cold dark streets at 2am, he didn't notice in the darkness that he had eerie bloody dripping down his fangs. He left a trail of blood drops directly from the river to his hideout! After all his efforts he didn't know that this one mistake would have let him to a catastrophe.

The trail of blood continued to ooze. Even by the morning, the blood was still as fresh as a newborn baby. Due to the sunlight in the morning, the blood seemed ever so bright red and clear. The drops were clearly visible and showed.

Chapter 25

Mistakes And Regret

Location:Royal Edinburgh Hospital

Time: 9th August 2016

It was a dark rainy day; the eerie sky

was crying down with rain. Ellie had arrived in her flat, which had only consisted of a living room with a little kitchen, a bedroom and a bathroom. There wasn't enough facilities, but it was decent for one person. After she made her dinner, which was the usual Pasta and ground turkey, she turned on the TV to watch Keeping Up with the Kardashians' and after the show, when Ellie was about to turn off her television, an advert about mental illnesses came on. In the first 5 seconds of the advert, it caught her attention and she was intrigued and was eager to find out more about it. The advert showed pictures of a brain, which had been affected by a mental illness. The advert was trying to persuade the viewers to donate money to the research of mental illnesses and to get medicines for the people, who have been affected by illnesses.

All of a sudden, it dawned upon Ellie that she had done something wrong that could affect someone else's life and by wasting all that money on Tom, it wasn't worth it and even when he didn't actually need it. Then she had a flashback to the hospital, she remembered lying to the receptionist and the guilt that came with it. She remembered all of the children, whose life has been ruined by that illness. This made Ellie realise that she should do something that would stop all of this, otherwise karma would hit her! With fear and tension filling up in her body, she couldn't sleep all night.The only thing she could think about all night, was the lives that were ruined by her. After lots of thinking, she finally knew what to do and that was to tell the truth.

Without thinking about anything, she picked up the phone because she thought it was a good idea to try and persuade her boss to stop everything. She did not want to do this anymore and she wanted to save lives which is what a real doctor should do; all the the guilt was building up.

"Hello, Blood Spirit. It is me Ellie and I want to tell you something." she said.

"If you are trying to stop me, it's not going to work, " said a deep voice on the other side of the phone "Remember our deal and if you don't I give you trial."

She remembered the deal; she didn't want to die but she didn't want to help someone, who was so vicious, become so powerful and this was all the fear that when he became powerful he would crush Ellie and so many people will die.

"Yes, I do but isn't there another way that we could do this?" the doctor asked, sounding worried.

"No, I expect this done!" The line went dead.

What could she have done now? She could tell someone, but who? She couldn't have told Kylie or Audrey- what would they do? She could tell George maybe, we could have come up with a plan to save Kylie. Kylie was what Blood spirit wanted after all. "But why does Blood spirit want Kylie?" she asked herself "Who would know?" She was senile and wished that she didn't get herself involved in this problem.

Ellie then thought of George, Kylie's adoptive dad. He would know of anything that would be so powerful that Blood spirit, the most feared villain, would want. Expeditiously, she set off towards George's house and she knew that even if George didn't have the answer she could always go to speak to Kylie herself.

Chapter 26

Daughter Love

Location:Hospital, The safe house

Time: 10th August 2016

George was still extremely ill, but he had signs of recovering. He was missing Kylie a lot but he didn't know why. He pressed the help button and a nurse came in.

She looked at George and asked her, "Yes, how may I help you?"

George told the nurse to bring him his phone. She said that is not possible because George was not fully recovered. He did not agree and was about to get up when the nurse said she will give him the phone for a little while.

She brought him the phone and then George called the agent, who took Kylie to the safe house, and told him to bring her to the hospital since he was recovering. The agent agreed and brought Kylie to the hospital.

George was waiting for her for an hour, then he saw her face coming through the door and a great big smile came on his face.

He faintly said her name and was trying to sit up but Kylie said "Dad, don't!"

When George heard the word Dad coming from Kylie's mouth, he felt an emotion he hadn't felt for years. It was love! Water started to build up in his eye, he started to cry with joy.

With all the love she has showered on George in the past couple of weeks, George couldn't let anything happen to her. She had become a part of George's life. If she went, George would turn into a dull and upset man. George was so happy about when she called him Dad. He had told her when he came out of hospital, they'd live like a real, happy family.

After being called Dad, George decided to gift her with favourite book, therefore

he asked the agent to go to the bookstore
and buy it for her. Her favourite book was
Alice In Wonderland. It was stolen at the
care home, but she never asked for it as she
was too polite to ask for it . Consequently,
this would have been a perfect present for
Kylie but George also gave her a

Even after everything, George still had
a guilt feeling in his heart. He felt that
what he had done very wrong when he had
been lying to Kylie and telling her that he
was going to work in the Baked Potatoes
Shop, when he was going to the MI5. In
addition to that, the main reason he got
Kylie, was to complete the mission and
catch Blood Spirit but during the mission
he started to created a bond between the
two. So he looked at Kylie held her hands
and said sorry for everything he has ever

done.

George asked the agent to bring the envelope that he had kept safe with him. It was the adoption papers for Kylie, but he hadn't signed them because he never knew he was going to keep her but now he has created a bond, he wanted to be Kylie legal father and since he only had a year until his retirement, he wanted a family to spend his retirement with.

When George asked this question, she did not want to answer it because she was nervous and didn't know what to say.

Then George continued he said "Just to get things straight, I haven't told you about my family, but I have to get it clear, I used to have a wife called Kate and a son called Harry.They meant the world to me and Eddie knew that too.I was on a mission and I had to capture Eddie and to weaken me, he killed my wife, my son and my unborn son, who was 8 months. It was my fault they died and I did not want that to happen to you and I couldn't lose you as well and to Blood Spirit. I wouldn't be able to live and after meeting Kylie and keeping her this family may have forgiven him."

He believes that all the guilt behind his family was gone.

"I think that me losing my family and unfortunately your parents abandoning you, was fate. Fate knew our lives were miserable and that is the reason we were brought together, we all have to have someone to lean on or help and that is why me and you are together."

Kylie replies "I thought about that too,

before you came into my life, my life was miserable, my roommate Electra use to bully me about the way I am and after you have come i have been more happy. I don't even remember my parents but you have been a better dad than both of them."

"Before we leave, we have to wait for the doctor to discharge me and I know the reports will be positive." George said.

George and Kylie waited until the the reports came, but unfortunately the reports said that George wasn't allowed to be discharged for another two days because if he moves his knee they may snap and he won't be able to walk for the rest of his life. George couldn't refuse but Kylie did not want to leave her father, so she stayed with him.

Chapter 27

The Mad Plan

```
Location:George's House

Time: 12th August 2016
```

George has just managed to relax on his sofa, when he heard knocking on his front door. It was Ellie who was coming to tell him the bad news.

After he opened the door, Ellie asked "Are you Kylie's adoptive father?"

"Yes, and you are?" He replied.

"My name is Ellie and I have come to tell you some bad, surprising news, which I have found out today." declared Ellie.

"I'm sorry, about what?" inquired George

"About Kylie." Answered Ellie.

"Come in, " said George, inviting her into his semi-detached house.

Curiosity was building up inside George, alongside fear as to what happened to Kylie.

"What about her?" asked George?

"She has something, which a dangerous man is after and if he gets it, he will be the most formidable man in the world." exclaimed Ellie.

Ellie, had been given tea and custard

cream biscuits by him. Custard creams were her absolute favourite but she was here to talk to George about something very serious about Kylie.

"Kylie has some amazing talents, which are controlled by her mind, which you thought were a mental illness." explained Ellie

"And the man wants these powers because he wants power?" Asked George.

"He wants more power, he is the most famous evil mastermind in the world!" Ellie says, emphasizing the word more'.

At this point, George looked really puzzled, "I don't really understand, how the man will..."

"His name is Blood Spirit" interrupted Ellie.

"How will Blood Spirit get the powers?" asked George.

211

George was awfully confused, therefore Ellie had reiterated it in more detail, "Kylie has some amazing talents, which are controlled by her mind, which you thought were a mental illness." explained Ellie. "I was set up as a fake doctor to make sure that Tom gets closer to Kylie. Then when Tom was close to Kylie, I would take a sample of her DNA so we can analyse it to recreate the cells."

"But what would happen when the DNA runs out so you can't recreate it?" asked George.

"Blood Spirit was planning for me to kidnap her and take her to his secret lair." Said Ellie.

As soon as this sentence had processed in Georges brain he looked crestfallen.

"What can we do to stop this plan?"

asked George

"Well, we can tell the staff at the hospital, so they can remove him from the ward,
" proposed Ellie.

As they walked into the hospital, Ellie
dressed as a doctor and George beside her,
confidently they walked up to the desk to
meet one of the patients.

"I would like to see the head doctor
of the mental illnesses department." demanded Ellie.

"May I ask why?" asked the receptionist.

"I need to discuss the well-being of one
of the patients." answered Ellie.

"OK, just through there." she said,
pointing towards the door.

They decided to talk to the hospital
staff and tell them what's happened, so

they could get evidence to reveal that Kylie doesn't have a mental illness.

"So, Dr Ellie how do we know you are telling the truth." Inquired the head doctor.

"I was the one, who recognised the symptoms that Tom had to get him into the hospital" said Ellie "Check your records, if you don't believe me!"

"Can I see some more evidence?" asked the doctor

She then pulled out her phone "On here I have recorded Blood Spirit, the mastermind of this plan, telling me the idea."

After the video, the head doctor said "Ok, we will have Tom removed immediately from the ward."

Chapter 28

Crime Cases

```
Location:Court

Time: 15th August 2016
```

In the morning Basima woke up and got ready. She was all prepared for the trial and she felt determined that she was going to win her court case! John was very grumpy and didn't have much energy however he was also sure he would win. He didn't need to put any energy in this fight, he felt like it was all in his hands. After a few hours, they went to the trial and everyone took their seats. The trial had begun!

"Your Honour, I have some evidence that will prove that Mr. John Sadiq is the guilty party! Take a look at Mrs. Sadiq's arms, she has bruises and cuts all over her, due to the violence of Mr. Sadiq. I can prove that these marks were caused because of Mr. Sadiq due to this broken glass, which comes under Act 40001-40703 of Violence Of Women. This broken glass was smashed from the window that leads to the back garden of their house, labs have examined and checked, and the window material matches, which proves it was from there, and the fingerprints are of Mr Sadiq, and the DNA reports prove that the blood on the glass is of Mrs. Sadiq and that this glass was cut on Mrs. Sadiq." the solicitor explained.

"NO!" John became very violent and angrily started screaming and shouting across the room, throwing everything everywhere and acting insane.

"Your Honour, as you can see, the opposite party is acting extremely horrifically, and you can tell that he obviously does worse than this in front of his wife and his young children, " she continued.

Due to the fact that John didn't have any additional proof or any solicitors to back him up, that he didn't abuse his family, he was sentenced to 5 months in prison. When he found out that he was going to prison, his face dropped and poured into tears because he thought he didn't do anything wrong. Katie had a smirk on her face and was glowing with buoyancy; whilst Tom and his mum were filled with mixed emotions. Mum felt this was a good decision for everyone and everything would finally change and her family would be in a safe environment, but she knew that she still loved John and would dearly miss him, but at the same time, she knew he deserved the punishment.

While everyone was in the court, mum thought it would be wise to get a divorce with dad at that same time, as it would be beneficial for her and the kids. She knew that without him living in her house, there would be no drama at home and every-thing would be okay. She interrupted the jury and asked for a divorce. However, dad didn't agree to it. Even though he didn't agree to it, mum needed some time away from him and she didn't want any contact with him. But then she thought about the kids Tom and Katie would both need help when they are older, and she knew that she couldn't look after the kids by herself. Consequently, she asked for a separation, in which everyone was happy to do.

This was a very hard day for everyone, as dad was sent to jail, mum had to look after two children by herself, mum and dad got separated and the children had no dad to rely on for half a year. What else could go bad? It was that one day where Katie and Tom had to experience their dad go to jail. They had to sit through all the pain and watch the devastation. This was also a moment never to be forgotten.

Chapter 29

Self Harm

```
Location:Tom's House

Time: 18th August 2016
```

A week after dad was sentenced to 5 months in prison, mum had to visit him regarding Tom's anxiety. Mum was agitated to visit him but it had to be done for the sake of Tom. That Monday morning, when Kate and Tom were busy, mum went to dad for advice.

"I'm not here to meet you, I'm just here for Tom's sake. I need to know what to do for Tom's anxiety, well I'm not sure if it's anxiety but I'm pretty sure it is." mum muttered, not really wanting to look at him.

In an angry tone, dad asked what made mom think that he has anxiety. At this point, mum knew that the tension and heat was rising.

Mum worryingly exclaimed, "Well, I think it's due to the fact that he has marks on his arms, he could be self-harming, you need to be perturbed about it John, he's our son and we need to take care of him!"

Snipingly, dad said, "Well it isn't my fault that I've been taken away from him and I have never spent time with him."

Mum got furious but remained calm and didn't reply to that comment.

Mum wanted to end the feistiness, so she ended it by asking for advice on what to do. He thought that Tom was doing all this for attention, so he didn't care.

Mum argued back and said, "Why would he do this for attention? He has marks on his hands and he looks depressed most of the time. Plus I don't even blame if he wants attention because he hasn't been with us for some time of his life. Anyways you never care about him, not even Katie, no one, you have never cared about our family, all you care about is yourself! You have a rotten, deficient, negligent personality and that will never change about you! Did your father treat your mother like this? You will never be a good father, you're self-centered, selfish person! I hope you decompose in prison and have a good time, I'm done with you, bye!"

Mum needed to get away from dad and everything which surrounded her, so she decided to go for a walk. But instead of walking, in the corner of her eye, she saw a man who was a drug dealer and he offered her some weed. Moronically, mum took it, without realising what she was going to do to herself. A few moments after, she felt weird and fainted. No one knew she had fainted as she wasn't in a local area. Luckily, an elderly man, in his nineties, found her and rang the police straight away. Several hours later, she found herself lying in the hospital bed. She ran out of the hospital not realising what had happened to her and continued to smoke weed.

When mum arrived home, she was reflecting on what has happened over the past few years. She thought she was a terrible mother, wife, daughter, and raised a family vacuously. She just wanted everything to be okay and normal but maybe that would never happen. Her attention came to Tom and everything changed immensely. Who knows what will happen? Then she thought about Tom and how his life would be when he grows older, his high school, friends, and adult life. Then she thought about Tom's anxiety and what caused it. Could it have been anything to do with the family's history?

Chapter 30

The Doc Dies

```
Location:Hospital

Time: 24th August 2016
```

On a sunny day, Ellie was walking down from the hospital not noticing her surroundings. She was joyfully strolling down the path; birds were tweeting, the wind was humming, the flowers were dancing. She was thinking about how vigorous her life was. Within a blink of an eye, Tom and Blood Spirit were standing in front of her looking rather resentful. She knew something was going to happen soon but she wasn't sure what. Her facial expression showed that she was inquisitive about what was going to happen and why they came up to her, but she was an audacious person, so she was prepared to face them.

"Stop right there Ellie!" roared Tom

Ellie stopped but was curious of what they were both going to say. They were talking in an aggressive tone- she knew something had happened!

"What happened, why do you seem so angry?" Ellie questioned Tom.

Blood Spirit intervened within their conversation and told her to stop being innocent. Ellie knew what they were going to talk about but acted as if she didn't. It was vitally important for her not to give any hints or clues to both boys otherwise her plan would be ruined. She was trying to be innocent and not to give anything away.

Blood Spirit was discombobulated, he believed that the doctor was planning something against them and may reveal the secret to everyone but he did not want to blame her if she wasn't going to, so Blood Spirit came up with an amazing scheme

229

to guilt trip the doctor to reveal her plans. The doctor had a timid face, drops of sweat were racing down from the top of his forehead down to the neck. The doctor was too nervous and when Blood Spirit tried to guilt trip her, she did not crack. She did not want to say anything because she hadn't done anything bad and she wanted to be a good doctor.

But Blood Spirit wasn't a good guy, he recalled the conversation where the Doctor was blackmailed by Blood Spirit.

"This is my bad side of me and my other side is even worse, you don't want to face the other side of me."

The Doctor was getting even more hesitant, she did not want to get killed.

Blood Spirit did not have the patience, he did not want to take the chance to go in prison. He gave the doctor a last chance to spill the buzz but the doctor refused. Ellie pulled a BB gun by accident and she started to laugh but then Blood Spirit got his gun

BANG!!

The doctor was on the floor, blood pouring out her head. Then Blood Spirit grinned and walked away into the shadows.

Chapter 31

Back-Stabbing Brother

```
Location:Tom's House

Time:25th August 2016
```

A few days after the court hearing and

dad going to prison, Tom started wondering how the court received enough evidence to send his dad to jail. He wondered who would snitch up his dad like this and break his family apart. As Katie pretended to feel sorry for Tom, she sniggered behind him as she thought she had completed a part of her mission and she was going to get promoted, her dream was coming true. But Katie wasn't clever enough and she hadn't covered up her tracks so perhaps Katie wouldn't get her promotion after all...

Tom had seen and heard Katie sniggering, which only led to one thing...she was the culprit! Tom was shocked, although, he had also doubted her in the first place- when she said she was his sister (as he had never seen her before) nor had his mum mentioned her. A few hours later, Tom was thinking about how he could get his own back on Katie, seeing as she was a stranger that had been living in the house and she had stitched up Tom's step-dad for abusing his mum. As Tom thought to himself he knew that he was the only man for the job and that nobody else would help him and he would not want anyone else finding out about it, just in case they get enough evidence to prove that he's a murderer and that he framed Katie for the murder. All Tom had to do now was get a knife from the kitchen, without being caught and leaving the house without being seen. Midnight had arrived, Tom had his black gloves on and his balaclava which was covering all his face. He was waiting for somebody to pass by. Tom didn't want to do this but he knew it was for a good cause and he wasn't going to be caught for the murder because he was going to frame Katie. A lady was walking past him, he took the chance- he grabbed her from behind and digged the knife in her back, she fell on the ground, with blood dripping everywhere, Tom ran as fast as he could before he got caught.

Tom sprinted as fast as he could through the streets and didn't stop until he came outside the house. He heard a car door. Looking both ways and until it was clear, he ran inside and started shouting

"Hello, hello anybody home?" Nobody replied.

He bolted upstairs as fast as he could, and planted the evidence in Katie's room, so she could be framed for this murder; he hid the blood dripping knife under her mattress and hastily put the balaclava and gloves in the next door neighbours bins, otherwise he might have been caught as his fingerprints were printed on the clothing. As Katie arrived home, Tom was lying on his bed reading a magazine.

When Katie went to her room and found blood on her carpet she screamed "AAH-HHH!".

Tom walked into the room, "What have you done? And where have you been, you have come home really late tonight. I need to inform the police about this, you aren't getting away with a crime!"

He called the police and told them everything.

"I need police at number 33 Uxbridge Road UB2 J5F as soon as possible, I have found a murder weapon, and the room that it's in is full of blood, please help me!"

A few minutes later somebody banged on the front door, Tom ran downstairs and opened it. The police stormed inside.

"Where is the murder weapon and the murderer?" an officer shouted.

"She is upstairs! Come quick before she escapes with the murder weapon!" Tom screamed, leading them to Katie's room. The police bolted upstairs and found Katie sitting on the floor with the murder weapon in her hand.

"You're under arrest Katie Braxton, for murder, don't say anything or it may harm your defence as whatever you say will be mentioned in court".

She was perturbed and perplexed- she knew her mission was a fail. She wasn't going to get promoted and she was definitely going to be sent to prison. Her life was over for being an agent. What was she going to say to Kylie?

Katie was shocked about what was happening. She looked around the cell trying to figure out who would frame her. She wanted a say to what had happened to her. She knew that she was framed by somebody, but did not know who. She couldn't get her head around it, she was one of the top agents in the country and somebody had tried to frame her and they had accomplished their task!

She knew she had to do something about it because she couldn't live in prison for 5 years for something that she didn't even do!

After several minutes of wondering who would do such a thing, she saw Tom in

the corner and wondered why he was here,
she had a suspicion on him. Tom was a
very clever person, he thought he would
never going to get caught for what he has
done, but he didn't know what kind of
person Katie was because she was a total stranger to him. Tom was smiling and
Katie started getting aggressive; she was
strained onto the floor, put in handcuffs
which was attached to the door handle.
They both looked at eachother and Tom
gave a cheeky smirk.

Chapter 32

The Truth Is Out

Location:George's House

Time: 27th August 2016

"There's something I need to tell you." said Katie

Katie was calling from the police sta-

241

tion as she had to tell Kylie that she had been framed. If she didn't, she would lose 5 years of her life and her job! Katie told Kylie to meet her at St Leonard's Police Station urgently so she could explain everything. Kylie was confused and didn't know what she was doing at the police station. Had she caught Tom and sent him to jail? Kylie didn't think that was a likely story but she couldn't think of anything else. As soon as she could, she slipped on her shoes and quickly drove off to the police station.

At the police station, there was a terrible shock for Kylie. Katie was in jail instead of Tom. She wondered how she got herself in jail and angrily asked Katie. Katie explained everything from how the police officers came and took her to jail without listening to what she had to say to when Tom had sniggered at her. Kylie was very frustrated at this and wanted to know how Tom had outsmarted them so easily. Kylie then remembered the time when Katie had shown him the recording of Tom's parents fighting and started to piece things together. Tom really didn't have an illness...he was just faking it. Since Tom had seen Kylie's powers, he had started to act very strangely. Was Tom doing this all for attention and because he had been influenced by his parents? Even if he was, Kylie was very angry and had to get revenge on Tom.

As well as that, Katie had told Kylie about Tom calling someone secretly and meeting with someone. Katie became very suspicious and was trying to figure out who

Tom was secretly talking to when he had framed her. Kylie only had one question in his head...who could it be? He had to know who this person was and what connection they had to Tom. It was a mystery. Kylie knew that there still was someone on the loose, who was also part of all this mess and maybe that person was also on the same mission that Tom was doing and that person might have been helping him.

Katy interrupted Kylie's thoughts and said, "Ellie was also a double agent but she was on our side. She deceived Blood Spirit and told us the plan. When you suspected him, it turns out you were right...he was caught talking to Tom on the phone and Tom had been slipping off every day claiming he was going for a checkup but he was really going to see Blood Spirit. I'm not sure if he was forced to do this and was blackmailed.

"Or he might have been working for the guy that Tom was talking to." Kylie muttered to herself.

"This is outrageous, I'm going to go teach Tom a lesson." Kylie boomed.

She had to have a word with Tom, he was just getting out of control. Kylie could not, under any condition, let Tom win this battle and she had to get Katie out of jail since she was innocent. Katie had been blamed for something that she didn't do whilst she was on a mission for Kylie, so Kylie had to make it up to her and she had to do something as soon as possible. Kylie didn't care about picking up anything to defend herself and she didn't take anyone with her. She just angrily stormed off to Tom's house to have a strict word with him.

Chapter 33

World War III

```
Location:Tom's House
```

```
Time: 27th August 2016
```

Kylie rushed towards Tom's house and flounced towards the door. She hit her fist on the door as hard as she could several times and screamed at the top of her voice whilst the side of her fist bled.

"TOM OPEN THE DOOR RIGHT NOW BEFORE I CALL THE POLICE!"

Tom, from the other side of the door, was bewildered..."Who could that be on the other side of the door? Had someone got confused between him and another Tom?" Although this was quite unlikely, he tried to believe that it was true. Slowly, he walked down the stairs and opened the door. As soon as he opened the door, a torrent of words hit him.

"TOM...YOU ACTUALLY TRIED TO KILL YOUR OWN FRIENDS?! THE PEOPLE WHO TRUSTED YOU! WHY WOULD YOU!?"

"WAIT!" Tom shouted so loud that even Kylie's voice couldn't be heard. "What

are you on about?!" Tom acted all innocent and tried to oppose whatever Kylie
was saying but then after that, he finally
had to give in and laughed as he told Kylie
everything.

"You really thought I was going to be
the one left out when everyone else got attention and I didn't? I want to be the
main one, I had to do so much to try to
achieve my goal...from framing my sister
for a murder that I did, and convincing
Audrey to kill himself."

"You did what?" Kylie was more shocked
than when she came in.

"Yes, you heard me right...I framed my
sister and I convinced Audrey to kill himself. I am a mastermind!" Tom said this
with a huge smirk on his face that made
Kylie so angry that she wanted to murder

Tom right there and then.

Kylie was so surprised that her mouth was open as wide as it could go. Fortunately for Kylie, she had caught everything that Tom had said on her phone as she had recorded every single thing. Sneakily, she sent the recording to the police, who then received it a few seconds later. As soon as the police received this information, they rushed quickly to Tom's house and started knocking on the door. Tom showed Kylie a gun and then she knew if she spoke she would be killed. Luckily however, the police came and forcefully arrested Tom while he was screaming and punching the officers. Then they took him to the police station and Kylie went with them for evidence.

At the police station, Tom tried proving

himself innocent however he failed miserably as the recording was played in front of him and the police. The recording showed every single word Tom had said. The police all shook their heads as they told Tom that he was going to be sent to jail without a trial as there was enough evidence to prove him guilty, but no evidence to prove him innocent. Tom tried to prove himself right, however he knew no matter how hard he tried, he knew he would fail. Tom started to think...what about Blood Spirit? He had failed his mission...he led Tom to being sent to jail...Blood Spirit had to go to jail too...

He had one chance to prove himself innocent...he exclaimed loudly.

"It was Blood Spirit... I hired him and he's the one who's trying to kill Kylie and

Audrey."

He hoped this would work but it just
made the police angrier as they found out
that Tom had hired Blood Spirit. Tom's
plan had failed. Meanwhile, Kylie was just
wondering who that mysterious person was
that Tom used to meet and talk to on the
phone...and then realised that it must have
been Blood Spirit as Tom had just said
it himself. Kylie thought to herself...there
still was a mission that had to be completed - Blood Spirit had to be sent to
jail. As Tom was going into his prison cell,
in which he would rot for his lifetime as
he had been sentenced for a life imprison-
ment, he saw his fake sister coming out of
jail. After a few seconds of wondering how
his sister was there, he realised that what
he had said in the recording had proven

her to be innocent and she had been released from jail.

As she was passing him, she gave him
a smirk and whispered the words in Tom's
ears.

"I told you I'll get you back."

As she said this, she strode off leaving
Tom regretful. Before he stepped inside
his prison cell,

Kylie loudly said, "Go to jail."

Tom was puzzled...what she was talking
about? Soon, memories of the monopoly
game came into his head and he realised
that Kylie was talking about when he went
to jail in the game. Tom closed his eyes
and sighed...there was nothing he could do
now. His life was over. At that moment,
Kylie got a phone call from George to come
to the hospital.

Chapter 34

Safehouse

```
Location:MI5 hideout

Time: 1st September 2016
```

"The reports have come back in. You're recovering but you need to be more careful. No more M.I.5 for a long time!" said the doctor cautiously.

"When can I go home though?" Inquired George.

"I would recommend you to not go right
away however you can go if you want to.
It's entirely your choice sir" replied the
doctor, who very clearly wanted George to
stay.

"I'd like to go to home, please" answered
George.

"Ok" replied the doctor "But and this
is important, you will need to take plenty
of rest".

"Thank you, and yes doctor I will."

"Can I just call someone to collect us?"
asked George.

"Ok, but quick" replied the doctor, who
then left.

"Who are you going to call?" asked

Kylie.

"Some Security." replied George.

"OK." said Kylie.

1 hour later, a metallic blue Auto Rick-shawi. A man got out with 2 others, all wearing black suits and black bow-tie with handguns. They had an M.I.5 badge on the suits so it was clear that this was the "security".

"How are you George?" asked one of the agents.

"Good, Good!" replied George.

"This must be Kylie then." Pointing at Kylie.

"Yes!" replied Kylie.

"Give me your bags and we'll take you the rubble." said one of the others.

"What is rubble?" enquired George?

"Your house, Blood Spirit blew it up,

didn't you know?"

"NO! why didn't anyone tell me?" said George as a tear dripped down his eye.

"Can I just phone someone to collect us?" asked George.

"Ok, but quick!" replied the doctor, who then left.

"Who are you going to call" asked Kylie.

"Some Security" replied George.

"OK" said Kylie

1 hour later, a metallic blue Auto Rickshawi. A man got out with 2 others, all wearing black suits and black bow-tie with handguns. They had an M.I.5 badge on the suits so it was clear that this was the "security".

"How are you George?" asked one of the agents.

"Good, Good" replied George.

"This must be Kylie then." Pointing at Kylie.

"Yes" replied Kylie.

"Give me your bag's and we'll take you the rubble" said one of the others.

"What rubble?" enquired George.

"Your house, Blood Spirit blew it up, didn't you know?"

"NO!, why didn't anyone tell me?" said George, a tear dripping down his eyes.

An Auto Rickshaw is quite a fast car, and was able to reach the house quickly. In the car George had started to cry. Kylie remembered his wife and children who were killed by Chamuel the killer. George's only memories of them were in his house which was now nothing but rubble.

When George reached the house, he started to cry a lot. He had lived in that house for

20 years. The only thing Kylie could do was to try and comfort him by telling him it's all right and everything was going to be okay as he didn't have to stress about anything and don't worry be happy-quoting Bob Marley one of George's favourite artist.

In the rubble, George found a shattered frame with a photo inside. It was George with his wife and children. He showed Kylie and then went they with the agents to a safe house while M.I.5 tried to find George a new house. The safe house was massive. There were a lot of spy gadgets in a secret room in the bathroom. In the garage there was a Aston Martin Vanquish. It was bigger than the other house. There were many other people, all in M.I.5 who were talking about what had happened. An agent took Kylie away to the hall where there were a lot of things to do like playing a game on the PS4 (which Kylie wasn't interested in) and to read a book. Kylie read Alice in Wonderland, one of her favourite books since a small age. Elektra stole her only copy and sold it in the orphanage. George brought her a new copy when he adopted her with the locket.

At the safe house, Kylie and George were sitting at a table. They were eating dinner. It had already been made by the chef. It was McDonald's. Kylie didn't like McDonald's as it was bad for her health and her lips. George had been keeping quiet ever since he had found out about what had happened to his house. He had only felt these emotions once before, when Chanmuel killed his wife and children. Kylie thought she knew what would cheer him up. Kylie saw a blueberry pie on a window ledge. With the flick of her finger, it landed on the table.

"How did that happen?" asked George shocked.

"I did that" replied Kylie

"How?" inquired George who had worked for 15 years in M.I.5, had never seen anything so bizarre.

"I don't know, I just can" said Kylie

"That might have been the reason Blood Spirit wanted to kill you" said Kylie.

"Really" said Kylie who had now gone very quiet.

"He thinks it's because of my illness" said Kylie a little while later.

"Nah, that's definitely not an illness" replied George. George already knew that she didn't have an illness he just didn't

Kylie to think that he knew.

"So, does that mean I've not got an illness" asked Kylie.

"Not sure, I'll do some research" said George.

Kylie had suddenly become happy. This could mean that she doesn't have an illness. She could have powers. George was sad. He had never realised that Kylie didn't have an illness. Even the doctors didn't realise. He decided that he was going to move to London after doing some research. The reason for this was in London there are more facilities for Kylie at the Great Ormond Street Hospital. He decided to buy a house there as well.

When he told Kylie, she was happy. Kylie had not liked Edinburgh and had always thought that London was a better place. George was still going to work in M.I.5 for another year at the headquarters in London. George was going to buy a brand-new house near Great Ormond Street Hospital. They moved to London the week after. Kylie's dream was to become a maths teacher and George finds a good college for Kylie to go to so that she can fulfil her dream.

Chapter 35

A Sister's Quest

Location:Hotel, Science lab

Time: 5th September 2016

The train finally reached at it's final stop, and Faith got off with her luggage and roamed around the windy cluttered streets of Glasgow until she found a suitable hotel - Riverside Homes, and she unpacked her things and began to plan her master plan. She thought about how she would distract everyone and make her way into the Dome. After a while, she had it all planned and was set. She couldn't back out now.

Faith jumped onto an eerie bus. Only one old lady was sitting there on a seat. Faith smiled at her as she sat down next to her. The lady gave her a piece of chocolate and Faith happily took it. She looked and stared at her. The warmth and love of the lady reminded her of her mother. A tear leaked, but this wasn't the time to be emotional. She reached at her stop; she went towards the door and looked back at the Faith. She smiled and waved as she went off at her stop. It was now only her in the bus and it felt quite weird and awkward. The bus took about half an hour to reach the woods, where the Lab Of Labs was. It was as if no one had ever come this way before, even the bus driver was staring at Faith he was smiling and sweating, looking worried. Faith took out her phone and looked at a baby picture of her and Audrey. She smiled and her inspiration was brought back. She switched her phone off, and reached her spot. She got off and the bus zoomed away in the distance, as she looked through the woods from a far distance and saw the Lab. She walked all the way to the big unknown science lab, the plan running wild in her blood.

Faith looked at the big bright crystal Lab from the outside. Everything looked so professional and neat. She had a slight feeling that not everything might go right. But she still had a hope in her heart that everything would go just fine, if she kept her eyes and ears open. She walked calmly towards the door and slapped her hand on her head.

"Oh shoot" she gulped.

"There's a high professional thumbprint scanner that lets you into the room! Ugh!" she thought for several minutes whilst hiding behind a flower pot. She then saw a scientist coming to enter the room; this was her chance.

She jumped from behind the pot and grabbed the scientist from the neck.

"Someone! Help! I can't breathe, who is this? Is this a joke to you? Security!!"

"I wouldn't call security if I were you"

she whispered gently into his ear, as he fainted due to Faith hitting a pressure point on the side of his neck.

"That's why karate rocks!"

A few minutes later, Faith entered the Lab dressed not as Hip Style Queen In Jeans' but Miss Faith, Senior Doctor And Scientist.' She watched all the scientists that were gathered around a table making the liquid medical cure. She overheard them saying that there would be an 89

"Hmmm" said Faith out loud, wells, a bit TOO out loud.

"Excuse me Ma'am!!" yelled one of the scientists.

"Oh pancakes!" she turned around and smiled, then almost made a run for it.

"Wait!" the old scientist boomed. "You don't get away that easily!"

He came up to her a dragged her all the way to the front in front of all the other scientists.

"This young scientist thinks it's alright to be loud whilst a mixture is being created, therefore she can do the hard job and take the medicine into the safe room!" he cackled.

"Ain't that right missy" he said all jolly like. "Here, take it, but be careful! And try to be a bit quiet next time, did you not learn in Science Uni that shouting whilst a mixture is being created can affect the particles and it makes the medicine come out totally different?!"

"Um, yes sir, sorry sir" she muttered, then gave a cheesy smile.

"Call me Josh, haven't seen you around much, eh? Careful, HOLD IT CAREFULLY!"

he screeched. "Okay enough chitchat hurry up and put that priceless valuable in the safe room. Let's all have party fellas, we're rich!"

Faith rushed out of the room quickly, but carefully.

"Jheez, I think he has a bipolar disease too, he's just like Audrey, one minute jolly next minute fierce, like a cat to a tiger!" she sighed.

"Please please, please make this work!!"

She galloped to the store room and locked herself in, safely clutching to the medical cure. It was full of all different sorts of medicines, shrinking, growing, flying, turning into an animal, you won't even believe.

"Oooooo!! A liquid for - Pancakes to Pop out Of Nowhere!" she took the liquid and open the bottle. She spilt it all over the floor and it was all shiny and green. She then smiled as she felt a bit dizzy and closed her eyes. In 3 seconds she opened her eyes and then boom! Pancakes!

She munched in delight and gobbled them all up as fast as windy flames devour.

"Hey! How long you taking in der!" said an unfamiliar voice, banging on the door.

"Uh oh!" Faith scrambled, and smashed the window with the plate of the pancakes.

"Arhhhh! Where's the mixture gone?" she looked all over, but she couldn't find it anywhere. There were too many potions and she felt like she was sinking in them all!

"Where's the mixture gone? Oi! Who's in there!! Josh Sir, Josh Sir, hey boss, there's an intruder in der!"

"Smelly daal flavour!" she saw the liquid rolling near a box and scooped it up.

"Hey!" she heard Josh, and now the scientist and him we're banging the door harder and harder and harder, its hinges were about to crack.

Faith quickly jumped out of the window, and howled as she cut herself because one of the broken glass pieces sticking out. She felt the world go weird and almost fainted, but then she thought about Audrey, and how much he had been through. She thought about how much she had already done for him. She couldn't give up now. Faith kept looking where she was going through her watery eyes. She kept praying and just closed her eyes-

BANG!

The door opened and Faith quickly jumped out. She fell flat down and rapidly got up and ran.

The alarm system's siren suddenly roared and was ear-piercing. Faith ran as fast as she could. It was like she was running from all the pain. And she wanted to let go of everything. Forget it all. Start again. She felt lost, hurt, as if nothing would ever become right again. She needed a shoulder to cry on. Someone to trust. She had no one. All the pressure was on her. She had no other choice. She nothing she could do. She was forced. She had to believe she could do this. She had to have faith, hope, this was her destiny. She wanted someone to share her feelings with, . But all she could do was, run. Run from everything. She ran from the monsters that captured her Audrey. She wanted to make this all better.

She ran onto the streets, they felt her pain. She dropped a tear whilst her blood was warm and pumping all over her body; it was like a flame fell onto the floor. Her legs crumpled as she just raced on, just for Audrey, he was all that mattered. She ran as she threw the lab coat into the bin and put the medical cure into her purse. She ran and ran. Everyone watched as she was alone, and she ran until she couldn't, until she had a stitch in her heart. She ran all the way to the toilets.

She rushed inside and washed the stinging blood off her arm, and put a fresh bandage on her. She looked at herself, and splashed her face with ice cold water, just like her heart. She drank sips of water and changed her clothes. She re-did her makeup. She re-applied her pink blush and hot red lipstick. She thickened her lashes and brushed her hair. She looked at herself, she felt proud. She picked herself back up. She smiled, and knew it would all be fine; she couldn't let anything break her now. She was like smashed glass, but she glued all the pieces by herself, and kept shining bright. She ran with hope all the way to Railway Trains Station, with hope that her brother could finally live his life the way he was meant to...

Chapter 36

The Last Phone Call

Location:Audrey's house

Time: 9th September 2016

RING RING

"Please pick up Faith you're annoying me now, this is the last time I can ever talk to you. If I don't kill myself now and wait for you, I know you will just stop me."

RING RING

"Pick up!!"

RING RING

At this point worry was flooding him, what could be more important than her own brother?

"Ahhh!"

"Heyaa its Faith"

"Yes finally about time. Faith I-"

"I can't talk right now but leave a message after the ting! Toddles!"

"WOW! Stupid voicemail!"

"Why isn't Faith picking up? And where she been for the past days?" He started crying deeply. "What could be so much more important that her brother, wait let me guess, everything to her!" "I know I hate her for what she did to me, and I will never ever accept her, but she is still my sister" He sighed as he sat down on the sofa.

Suddenly Audrey burst into gallons of tears. "She's left me again" he whispered as he crawled into a ball and hid in a blanket. He cried and cried and almost drowned in his tears. His older sister must have been sick of him again; chosen to leave him for good.

He finally realised trust is something that couldn't be earned back in a week or two. She was gone for 9 years and she came back in a week and he started trusting her. That was his pure mistake. He realised trust was something that his shop had ran out of; there was no more in stock.

"I know! I'll leave her a voice message, not everyone's like her and mum and dad who leave without say anything" he murmured, "I know how that feels".

BEEP

"Hey, um, Faith. I just wanted you to know."

He lowered the phone and gulped.

"How do I say this!" he thought

"Um Faith, I wanted you to know, I'm going forever Just don't worry about me anymore, no one should worry about a dead body, they're gone anyway, you should know that the dead cannot rise again. If I just leave this world everything will be better, no one's worried about me, so it's fine, goodbye Faith. And I want you to know, I haven't ever loved you. You haven't been a good sister, but it's fine. Bye Faith"

VOICE MESSAGE SENT

PRESS 1 TO DELETE

PRESS 2 TO HEAR YOUR MESSAGE

PRESS 3 TO RE-RECORD MESSAGE

PRESS 4 TO ADD ANOTHER MES-
SAGE

"I'm so sorry Faith"

Then Audrey begins to think if committing suicide is the best way to go. But
then another thought takes over' but no-
one will notice, they don't care about me
anyway'.. Audrey was on the verge of committing suicide. He had enough of fighting
the disorder, it had taken over him, he had
no control, no hope, so what's the point of
living anymore.

Chapter 37

Bipolar Disorder wins

```
Location:Audrey's house
```

```
Time: 9th september 2016
```

After sending a voice message to his

sister that had left him again, having his last conversation with her and anyone, depressed Audrey Tiller went into the small, cluttered, grubby garage and brought out a very old muddy yet strong rope with him into the garden. He felt the pale green wet grass swish past his feet as he was walking towards the tree that would be his deathbed. He chose the tall oak tree in his garden as he had many good memories with that tree therefore he wanted to die with something that meant thing in his life.

He lit up a massive circle of fire around the grand oak tree in his misty, pitch black garden so no one could stop him from what he would he would do next. He would finally be in his happy place, after having a bad life on earth. The flames were sinking into his skin as he felt the burning rays of heat on him. They marked his skin. He breathed heavily and inhaled all the smoke and thought about everyone he knew one last time. Audrey felt sad and depressed yet the time was about to come as he would meet his maker very soon.

He then tied the rope to the leafy oak tree's bare branch as hard and tight as he could, secure the rope. Then he breathed properly one last time and swallowed his last gasp of air from the cold breezy wind. He then wrapped the rope around his neck and closed his eyes. His heart was pounding as he was getting nearer and nearer death. His eyes were closing, his pulse rate was dropping by the second, could anyone stop him from doing this stupid act. He saw this bright light in the distance which disappeared with a few seconds of him passing away.

He stood on top of the cracked stool which he found in the bathroom storage.

"I'm sorry everyone. I'm so sorry Faith" he whispered to himself.

He could not undo this

He kicked the stool over.

His life was gone.

His soul was gone.

Forever. He could not undo this act. Audrey had now died and Bipolar Disorder had taken another life of a 21 year old.

Chapter 38

Everything's Gone

Location:Train Station, Hospital

Time: 11th September 2016

Faith reached Edinburgh and rushed down

the street from the train station. She flung the door open, full of joy, but when she arrived home she screamed, crying! It was dead silent. Nothing was heard, it was pin drop silence. She screams, longing for Audrey to come to her, running, hugging her hard.

She sat down, it felt so cold, as if no-one had been in here for years. She saw the three miss calls from Audrey and a voice message. She instantly felt a weird pain in her tummy and because she was so worried she threw her phone in her bag and quickly went to look for her brother, totally forgetting about his voice-message.

"Audrey" She whispered his name, got up and started searching for him, screaming his name, too worried that she forgot all about the voice message.

She wiped her salty tears as she opened the creaky door and saw their old neighbour Ms. Jenny standing at the door. The old lady stood there, a tear rolled down her eye. She gave her an envelope full of 50 and a gold chain. Inside it was a card saying In Memory Of Audrey Tiller'. Faith's world seemed to deteriorate before her eyes. She lost all of her senses. Her heart sunk. Her face went pale. She couldn't believe this. Her brother, her only brother, was dead. Tears flooded her eyes.

She shrieked, she cried, she brutally hurt herself. She went totally insane; she couldn't take the pain anymore. She would never ever believe this until she saw Audrey's body with her own eyes herself. She sped all the way to Berryhill Hospital and Care and shouted, she called out for Audrey's name, not believing that her younger brother was dead.

The doctor came out of a very silent and colour-sucked room, and he slowly patted her and took her with him. Faith was taken into a room where Audrey's dead body was and their parents were sitting down crying their eyes out.

Faith sobbed and darted up to Audrey's body, crying in pain and screaming, madly talking to him about her journey on how she became a fake scientist, and stole an illegal liquid for him and she cut herself and bled. She wept and whispered for him to open his eyes.

"Faith, don't worry Hun, it will all be alright." her mother said to her warmly.

"No!" she shrieked. "This is all your fault! Woman like you don't even deserve

to have kids. All you care about is yourself. At least I left to fulfil a dream. YOU
left to LEAVE your kids, saying you're going on a holiday' you witch!" she teared
and felt like everything was broken.

Now she felt how her brother felt when
he wanted to commit suicide. She thought
about how her brother's life faded away.
He was distracted from his goals, lost.

"I wish you never existed, and then all
these problems wouldn't have been created. He's your SON not JUNK, but you
treated him like junk. You treat people
how you feel about them, you treated him
like junk, clearly you just feel that he's
junk. YOU CAN'T SAY YOU LOVE SOME-
ONE AND TREAT THEM LIKE THEY
DON'T MATTER AT ALL!"

"Darling, you know due to his awful

Bipolar disease this was expected." her mother sighed.

"WHAT ARE YOU TALKING ABOUT!!!!!? If you knew your own son would commit suicide because of his illness then why on earth did you leave him! You should have been a supportive mother! Why are you back now? Go away back from where you came from, you're going to show love to your when he's dead? You were never a good mother, and you won't ever be" Faith screamed.

Tears cascaded down her cheeks.

"Audrey was all I had! AUDREY! Please wake up! Audrey!!!! I need you!"

She continuously cried she had lost all her loved ones, she felt like no-one cared about her feelings; she was just another girl who no one cared about and just used.

Faith ran home weeping, uncontrollably thinking about whatever had happened for the past few weeks. She grabbed all her stuff and shut the house door behind her. She took the dusty golden house keys out of her ripped jeans pocket and mailed it to itself through the house door. She had no-one now, and nothing to do, no-one to go to and no-one to trust and believe in. She walked down the dark windy streets and threw her phone in the bin. Perhaps that was her last mistake she ever did to her younger brother. His last message remained unknown. She faded away in the distance, lost. She was indeed, Audrey's sister...

Chapter 39

The
Remembrance

Location:The church

Time: 12th September 2016

The wind was sighing and thrashing in

the treetops; the morning was cold and wet with a brisk wind sweeping the rain across the land. A curtain of rain beat down from the heavens. A flash of forked lightning and a great clap of thunder came close upon each other. Amongst the crowd where Kylie, Faith, George and some Ellie's family. Their faces were full of melancholy and despondency. Promptly, a long black car drove into the graveyard and in the coffin, was Ellie. The dark trees cast empty scary ghostly shadows over the deserted graveyard, the silence was deafening and tension hung in the air thickly. In the car window, was a bunch of bright flowers arranged to spell the words R.I.P Ellie. The driver got out of his car and opened the shiny black door.

With tears gushing down their faces, six

people picked up the dark stained cherry, a cushioned and quilted silky lining coffin. It was built with love to be the final resting place of one who had been so adored in their lifetime. It's faux-gold handles and polished sheen helped to reduce their distress of picking it up. They picked it up with care, knowing that someone close to them was being buried. Three men on each side, all wearing black, held the coffin with disquiet, with both hands on each side.

Slowly and gently, they placed the coffin dearly in the soil. The headstone was engraved with the words;

Here lies the body of Ellie Smith.

Rest In Peace.

Died 24th August 2016.

Died a hero's death in the hands of a

villain.

Everyone was sniveling, as one of their dearly, affectionate, loved one, had passed away. They hoped she rested in serenity in heaven, and she looked below at her family's action and protected them from evil. They would profoundly miss this faithful, staunch lady.

After the body had been buried in the soil, there was notable memorial service where a loving cherishing speech was given by the priest, Ellie's mum, and Kylie.

"On the 14th February 2017 Ellie died a hero's death in the hands of Blood Spirit. The same day Blood Spirit was caught and thrown into prison to rot. Ellie was a double agent who was on our side, she saved my life She will forever be missed and will always remain in our hearts. We all love you Ellie, rest your innocent soul in peace!" sobbed Kylie.

Walking into the church, full of melancholy, the family poured with tears, knowing that their beloved member, had been buried and could never be seen again. They opened the big rusty church doors and walked in with pain and agony where it was full of darkness and loneliness. They wanted to say a prayer for her before they left the church.

Her mum recited: "To my dear, beloved daughter, rest in peace, you will forever be missed and loved forever, stay blessed wherever you are, we will always think about you and visit you every day, you're the person who made my life better, and turned it into sunshine, I love you, rest in peace, amen." chapterChange Of Mind

Location:Tom's House

Time: 4th January 2017

After 5 months, dad was set free and
wanted to surprise his family. Despite that
he looked scruffy, he wanted to see his family as soon as possible. Although he had
made many mistakes in his past, he was
determined to sort them out; hence he wanted
to go to his house quickly. The only problem was that he had no way to get to
his house. The prison was all the way in
Blackford and he had to reach Gleneagles,
which was a long way. He tried to get hold
of a taxi but no driver would drive him as
he had nothing but 5.00. He was at the
verge of giving up and living on the streets,

but his family finally meant a lot to him, as a result, he walked all the way.

Walking for 3 hours, without any water or food, he finally reached his destination. With elation filling himself, he knocked on the rusty door and someone opened the door. It was Katie, with her phone on her ear. Her face descended with despondency and she dropped her phone with her mouth in the shape of an o' when she saw him.

Katie shouted at the top of her head and said "MUM, DADS HERE!"

Basima rushed downstairs and greeted him, even though she looked fairly scared. She told Katie to go downstairs and Basima and dad both went in the living room and slammed the door. As always, Basima was still was smoking weed, which was really bad for her, but still she needed it to help her with the stress, her kids tried stopping her, but she was an addict and she couldn't be stopped. She did not even feed her kids sometimes.

With fear oozing up her back, Basima and dad both sat down on each side of the room and mum started a conversation.

"How was it?" asked Basima.

"How was what?" answered dad

"Prison" Said mum

"Well my life was ruined for those 5 months but I have learnt from my mistakes, I guess." Dad sarcastically said.

Mum was shocked, and intrigued about what else he would say. Has he changed in the space of 5 months? Was going to prison good or bad for him? Did he finally care about his family? All these thoughts were going on in mum's head and she was eager to find out. Both mum and dad looked adamant to sort things out for their own reasons. They both spoke about the problems they have with each other and compromised to finally be a happy family.

After a few long hours of calm talking, they thought it would be beneficial if they forgot about the past and start afresh for many reasons. However, mum had flashbacks of when he hit her and that time when the kids got hurt- it kept coming to her mind as it was something never to be forgotten.

Dad, on the other hand, felt relieved to hit her and he wanted her to be scared of him. He thought fighting and abusing wasn't as bad as him going to jail, but mum thought the other way around. However, both feelings changed as they wanted to forget about the past and start new lives.

Mum happily said, "I think it's best to start again and pretend all this never happened!" despite she still had flashbacks of everything which had happened.

Dad replied, "Yes, it would do us all good, new start, new lives!" yet he couldn't forget what he had been punished for.

At that time, they both wanted best for their kids. However, they didn't realise Katie was behind the door listening to their conversation. She was gobsmacked to have found out that their parents had sorted things out because she didn't want them too. She wanted a family without dad. She indignantly stormed upstairs. Meanwhile, in the living room, mum and dad were talking about the children. Mum still had an instinct that something would soon happen to the kids if dad lived in the house, but she had to trust him if they wanted to have a fresh start. Although she was still frantic about this decision, she took a big risk in trusting him.

Immediately, dad said But Basima, I want to treat the step kids as if they were my own children!'

When mom heard this, she was scandalized! She also wanted dad to treat the kids as if they were his own, but who would have thought he would say that? Dad said he wanted to change and he did. Mum then spoke to dad and asked if he was feeling alright. She thought that prison had changed his life and he was finally a good, tender person who cares about people. After hearing that phrase, mum bought the kids downstairs and dad gave them a massive hug when he saw them. Katie wasn't enthused by it but she also felt he would be a better father. However, when Tom hugged dad, the whole atmosphere had changed. Everything has suddenly felt special. Mum felt contented again and Tom finally felt part of a family, but Katie obviously didn't care!

While Tom and Katie went in the kitchen, mum and dad have a noteworthy moment. Randomly dad said, I love you Basima!'

Mum replied, I love you too John!'

They both stood next to each other and dad gave mum a hug, after 7 months. This moment was also a memory to remember forever- when everyone reunited with each other! At this time, dad promised mum that he would never hit her again and that he would treat the family with care and devotion. Mum felt fully satisfied and felt as if she could trust John again. The family had gotten back together-what everyone was hoping for!

Chapter 40

Wrong Is Never Right

Location: MI5 Hideout

Time: 6th August 2016

There were three agents that had been

suffering from major problems. Jack, Scott and Marnie, during the fight when Blood Spirit tried to kill the agents. Jack was suffering from a severe concussion that had made him very confused as to what had happened to him as he was temporarily unconscious. Scott was suffering from breathing difficulties due to the fact that Blood Spirit had strangled him pretty hard. He couldn't breathe for one minute therefore for three hours he had breathing difficulties. Marnie, the newest agent at MI5, had internal bleeding as Blood Spirit had hit her stomach with a baseball bat and these victims had to be sent to specialist hospitals.

MI5 looked at the DNA on the agent's bite. MI5 had taken this bite very seriously as the member of staff that had been bitten on the arm, by an unknown person, was senior staff that had been part of the MI5 for over thirty five years. Amy, the senior agent, had been poisoned by the bite of the anonymous person therefore she didn't know who had bitten her as her memory was disappearing and she forgot who bit her. However, a DNA test would uncover who the terrible biter was.

Four hours later, the results came! Everyone at MI5 was shocked at the atrocious results. "it was BLOOD SPIRIT! Can you believe it!?" Said the DNA analysers.

Well the MI5 agents clearly were gobsmacked.

"How can Blood Spirit bite a human?" questioned Agent Julie, another senior agent to the DNA analysers.

"So, Julie it turns out that Blood Spirit

311

is a secret cannibal and he wanted to eat the flesh of Amy as he was feeling very peckish." said Robert, one of the DNA analysers, talking to the surviving MI5 agents.

Agent Amy was quite angry as she had been bitten therefore she had to get a cast and a sling for three months so, her bitten arm could heal. She would not be able to go to work for over two months. Also there was a chance that the poison in her arm could spread, get into her veins and reach into her blood therefore it could spread like wildfire. Amy disliked Blood Spirit very much and was annoyed at the fact that he bit her and she didn't catch him. After sulking for an hour, Amy realised that if she told the police he'd be imprisoned for physical assault therefore she had to file a complaint.

MI5 had been fairly angry with Blood Spirit as their staff were brutally injured after the disaster they had encountered but Jack, Scott, Marnie and a lot of other injured agents were going to get their justice. After agent Amy had filed a complaint, two hours later, the police came to arrest Blood Spirit in a van. He was being taken away .After bawling his eyes out, he was put overnight in a dark, dingy, claustro

phobic cell. He may have been released on bail if he gave one million pounds, but he didn't have that much money and was not going to be given one million pounds and so he wasn't going to be out of prison forever.

As no one would be generous enough to pay his bail, he had to stay in jail for his whole life. This issue was very serious as Blood Spirit was not a one of offender he was a multiple offender who has served a total of 5 years in his life. As his record isn't one of the best, his bail was very expensive and Her Majesty's Prison Edinburgh would not allow him as he had escaped many times therefore, he was confined in a solitary cell in a prison named HM Prison Shotts.

Agent Amy went to visit Blood Spirit in HM Prison Shotts, to tell him no one is paying his bail. He was very upset and begged for her forgiveness. But she did not accept it as she was still in pain and he biting her may have put her in a life threatening situation therefore why she would forgive him when he has brought nothing but pain and troubles into her life. Blood

Spirit has realised that he had made such a huge mistake but he also realised that it was too late and he would have to live in jail and die in jail.

Blood Spirit looked in the mirror. There was blood and bits of flesh all over his teeth. He had bitten Amy very hard. He had lost a tooth. He was going to regret this for the rest of his life. He was in prison and was going to stay there for life. His cellmate was called James. He had been been arrested for armed robbery. He went to Nationwide and stole all the money in the vault. He killed 5 police officers. He was the strongest in the prison much like Elektra in Kylie's orphanage. He had to go to the dentist, The dentist took out all his teeth and replaced them with dentures because all his teeth had cracked. Agent

Amy was wearing light-weight titanium armour which is as strong as titanium but light-weight. Blood Spirit was given a life sentence without parole.

In his first week he got into 3 fights. Everyone hated him even the prison workers, when he got into a fight they pretended to not notice till he was unconscious. He was a loner. He tried to get transferred but he wasn't allowed to. He would randomly start to have fights with people. No-one would talk to him. Everyone hated him because of what he did. He was going to rot in there for the rest of his life. *THE END*

Our Authors

Dilpreet Bains

I am 13 years old and my favourite author is Enid Blyton. I enjoy reading the Malory Towers series. My hobbies include singing and playing sports. This project has been very exciting and I have learnt many new skills.

Taranvir Chohan

I like reading books. My favourite book is Harry Potter and the Deathly Hallows and Roald Dahl's Matilda. My favourite hobby is to play on my PS4 and to read books. My favourite TV show is Timothy Goes to School. I really enjoyed this project as I was able to participate in a once-in-a-lifetime opportunity.

Avneet Dhesi

I am 13 years old and I am currently studying in year 8. My favourite author is J.K. Rowling and the book that I like is Harry Potter and the Chamber of Secrets. I am hoping to become a police detective when I am older. My favourite pets are dogs. This project has been a great opportunity for me and this will be great for my future.

Harnoor Ghuman

I am 13 years old and I love english and art. I also love reading. I like playing basketball and playing the keyboard. I was really happy and excited when I received this opportunity because ever since I was young I loved reading and writing. I wanted to be an author and I used to write stories. I always wished I could write a story and it could get published. Now that's finally come true!! It was a wonderful moment to enjoy and I absolutely loved it!

Jasmeet Khatri

I am 13 years old and I am studying in year 8. My favourite authors are J.K Rowling and Roald Dahl. I love singing and I aspire to become a singer when i am older. Reading helps me to be a bit calmer. I enjoyed trying to make the book funnier.

Amanjot Panesar

I am a 13 year old girl and I love reading. My favourite author is J.K. Rowling and I love the Harry Potter series. Some other book I like are the Divergent series (Divergent, Insurgent and Allegiant). This series is by Veronica Roth. I loved being a part of this experience as it gave me an opportunity to work as a group and write a book that may help me get a job in the future.

Jessica Sachdeva

I am 13 years old and currently study in year 8. I enjoy watching horror movies and my favourite series are the Harry Potter series written by J.K. Rowling. My hobbies are reading, visiting places and learning new things. I want to become a doctor or a forensic scientist when I get older as these jobs seem very interesting. Overall, I found this project a wonderful opportunity as it was a great experience and I hope to get further opportunities like this in the future.

Tegh Sandhu

I am 13 years old. My hobbies are playing football and listening to music. My favourite book is The Boy in the Striped

Pyjamas. I felt excited to participate in this project as at the end of it we will have a book that we wrote. I really enjoyed this experience and feel lucky to be picked.

Balmeet Sarna

I am a 13 year old boy and I love playing video games, listening to music and watching movies. Some of my hobbies are performing religious hymns, playing sport and playing instruments. Some books I like reading are the Harry Potter series, Monument 14 and Diary of a Wimpy Kid. I loved this project as it helped us by letting the creative beasts inside of us control our minds. This was a great opportunity and I will not forget it.

Manavee Sehdev

I am 13 years old. My favourite author is Roald Dahl. My favourite movie is Matilda. I loved this project as it gave me a great opportunity to write a book, which would be good for my future. I am hoping to become a forensic investigator when I'm older because I like investigation.

Harpreet Tatla

I am 13 years old and my hobby is football. My favourite author is David Walliams and my favourite story by him is Demon Dentist. This project changed me as a person and influenced me to read different genres of books. I felt very privileged to be picked to write this book.

Risan Thirupparan

I am 12 years old and I am studying in Year 8, I absolutely love reading. I have read many books and my favourite is the Percy Jackson collection by Rick Riordan. I also liked reading books by Marcus Alexander and Jeff Kinney. Some of my hobbies are playing table tennis, playing the violin and the piano. I loved this project because it made our minds think out of the box, it is something that I'll never forget in my life and it was a great opportunity for me.

19681123R00182

Printed in Great Britain
by Amazon